THE CIRCLE OF FIFTHS

ON BEHALF OF DEATH, BOOK 9

E.G. STONE

TARNEY BRAE CREATIVE ENDEAVOURS

For my menagerie

CONTENTS

Chapter 1   7
Chapter 2   19
Chapter 3   31
Chapter 4   43
Chapter 5   53
Chapter 6   65
Chapter 7   75
Chapter 8   87
Chapter 9   97
Chapter 10   107
Chapter 11   117
Chapter 12   127
Chapter 13   137
Chapter 14   149
Chapter 15   159
Chapter 16   171
Chapter 17   181
Chapter 18   191
Chapter 19   201

Acknowledgments   209
About the Author   211
Also by E.G. Stone   213

CHAPTER 1

We were out of popcorn, and I was crying. Yolanda patted my back awkwardly, her massive hands shaking my entire torso more than providing comfort. "It is over, Cal. The movie is over, you do not need to cry."

I was about to say that I wasn't crying because of the movie, but wracking sobs choked me and I could say nothing at all. Ever since I'd been reunited with my wayward soul, my emotions had been anything but steady. I found myself bursting into hysterical laughter at the most inopportune times—such as at the dentist. Other times, I was morose and dour, unable to find a positive word to say the entire day, even about coffee. Or, as it was that evening, I couldn't even watch a comedic movie without bursting into tears.

Baz, my cousin and the current Justice of Elsewhere, sauntered back into the room, holding a fresh bowl of popcorn. He froze as he saw the state I was in.

"What happened?" he asked, turning to Yolanda. "I left the room for five minutes!"

My rock troll assistant and friend shook her head. My pet miniature griffin ghost, Tempest, rubbed her head against my arm, sending shivers up my spine. I snatched a throw pillow from the couch and cradled it close to my chest. "He started crying as the movie was ending."

"We're out of popcorn!" I bawled, my tears smearing on the lenses of my glasses. Tempest clicked her beak at me and promptly flew to the other end of the room, obviously annoyed with my antics.

Baz bit back a snicker, shoved his ever-present sunglasses up his nose—a term of his position, as Justice is meant to be blind, though Baz could still see just fine—and threw himself onto the couch. "Well, you're in luck! I happen to have made a fresh batch. And there's a new episode of your favourite soap opera available, so we can watch that."

"Plus the new show where the foolish humans run into fire?" Yolanda asked hopefully. She'd recently become entranced with firefighter soap operas, and I didn't have the heart to tell her that it wasn't real, that it was just like the other drama shows we watched. Though, to be fair, I'm fairly certain she thought they were real, too. Baz just shrugged and reached for the remote. He waved the bowl of popcorn in front of my nose and I snatched it, dropping the pillow to the ground. My tears faded, and my uncontrollable emotions settled back into what was, for me, normal.

Death had said that this emotional unsteadiness would continue for a few months, but despite his cavalier statement, I couldn't help but notice that I wasn't left alone for a minute. During work hours, Agravane the aurai, my junior marketing agent, worked with Yolanda to make sure that at least one of them was in the room with me at all times. In the evenings, my girlfriend Neja often came over, usually bearing takeout and claiming that she worried I would starve, since I was incapable of cooking. The last few days, though, Baz had stopped by for a visit, declaring that he was on holiday and wanted to hang out.

I didn't believe any of their excuses for a minute. Death likely wanted an eye kept on me since I had absorbed his heart into me and now had more command over the powers of death than before. I was a Reaper already, but now I had slain gods and trapped Fate into a lonely prison. I was, in a word, dangerous. That, coupled with my unstable emotions, was wreaking havoc on my psyche. I tried very hard not to think about the consequences of my recent adventures. I often failed.

At the moment, my marketing work was shoddy at best. I'd managed to bungle a campaign for a nymph dance troupe, giving the bubbly pop group a decidedly more gothic feel than expected. (That they claimed they'd sold more tickets than ever was beside the point.) I had also started drinking tea at least once a day, which was sacrilege to my coffee habit.

Worst of all, I'd also forgotten to call my mother

twice in the last month, which was an Extremely Terrible Thing. She had, upon my remembering this obligation with abject panic, merely demanded I come for family dinner the next time I was in London. I had not been stupid enough to refuse.

Basically, ever since reuniting with my soul, my life had become a complete mess. I wasn't dying anymore, though, so at least there was that.

Baz, Yolanda and I watched more soap operas and ate more popcorn until I was insensate with exhaustion. When my soul had been on its own, I was rarely so tired. Now, though, I found myself nodding off almost as soon as it grew dark outside. That night, I fell asleep cradling the popcorn bowl, and listened to the quiet murmur of Yolanda and Baz hatching some terrible scheme. Finally, Yolanda relieved me of the remaining popcorn, claiming she was going to wash up. Baz peeled me off the couch and helped me to my room.

"I hate being like this," I grumbled, stumbling over my feet and trying to peer through my dirty glasses. "I want to be normal again."

"You will," Baz promised. "It's just going to take some time."

"I can't even do a proper social media campaign!" I flopped onto my bed, likely wrinkling my very nice trousers and cashmere jumper. I couldn't bring myself to even bother taking off my socks.

"Maybe you need some time off. A holiday, of sorts." Baz rolled me over so I was laying fully on the bed. "We can ask Death tomorrow. Maybe he'd approve a trip to Spain or something. You know, Aunt Teresa likes Spain."

"I'm not going on holiday with my mother," I muttered. The thought was terrifying, partly because my mother was terrifying.

Baz sat on the edge of my bed. "Yeah, you're probably right. I'm not sure I'm ready for that experience, either. You in swim trunks at the beach? We'd all be blinded."

It was true. I rarely got outside much, and when I did, it was usually overcast and I was wearing a three-piece suit. Except for my unfortunate time travelling adventure to Italy—where I'd first lost my soul, by the way—I had not spent much time in the sunshine.

"I want to be normal," I repeated into my pillow. Baz sighed and patted my shoulder.

"I hate to break it to you, cousin, but I think you lost normal a long, long time ago."

He was probably right.

Just as I was starting to contemplate that thoroughly depressing thought, hysterical laughter now building in my chest, my bedroom began to glow. Not the nice pleasant glow of a lamp on a rainy day, either, but the harsh white light of fluorescent bulbs in an industrial building.

I sat up, looking around. Baz shot to his feet, and I could almost see his eyes behind his sunglasses because of the light. "Uh, Cal...?"

"It's not me," I promised, standing also.

Before I could do something smart, like shout for Yolanda or call Agravane for help, music filled the room. Bad music. A high-pitched guitar wailed away, backed up by drums that were not quite on beat, a bass line that was certainly out of tune, plus a saxophone. There were words, too, but they were muted, a chant that was not quite intelligible and certainly did not fit the music.

The weird thing was, though, the music, minus the chanting, sounded familiar.

The light flared brightly enough to blind. I reached for Baz and he reached for me, each of us managing to hit each other—he caught me in the kidney and I got his ear—before we actually grabbed hold. The rest of the world seemed to fall away, leaving me with my stomach in knots, my lungs screaming for air in the worst possible way, and a splitting headache.

I squeezed my eyes shut and held on to my cousin, hoping that whatever this was, he would at least prove to me it wasn't a dream. Or a nightmare. I'd had many of those lately—ones that had me sitting straight up in bed, screaming—and didn't want any more. Most of them, I thought, were experiences my soul had gone through while wandering loose. That didn't actually make me feel much better about the dreams, to be honest.

Finally, the world seemed to solidify beneath my feet. My stomach was still roiling, but I could take a full breath. The light faded enough that I risked opening my eyes. What I saw only made my headache that much worse.

Baz and I were standing in a dimly lit room that looked like the storeroom of an unfortunately cluttered shop. There were broken chairs, squished boxes, and a whole host of other detritus that I couldn't identify at first glance, including what appeared to be the articulated skeleton of a chicken on a pedestal. Most of the stuff was pushed away from the centre of the room, where Baz and I stood in a circle drawn in red paint on the floor, surrounded by candles and random bits and pieces. A bowl with water, a feather, some sort of bones. Outside the circle were five people, four of them pale with either dark hair or blonde hair sticking up in impossible directions. These four wore black shirts, various pieces of metal jewellery, and copious amounts of eyeliner. Three were male, with one female, though they all looked of a piece. The fifth person was Black, and by far much neater, wearing a nice set of black trousers and a white shirt with the sleeves neatly rolled up, revealing tattoos done in white ink. The subject matter seemed to match the detritus of the shop, down to the articulated chicken skeleton.

Baz was the first to recover his manners and sense. "Hi," he said, giving a little wave. "What's going on?"

The smallest of the pierced and black-adorned people, black hair by far the most gravity-defying, let out a squeal. "It worked!" she said, throwing her arms into the air. American accent, very loud. So not likely we were in Britain, then.

"I told you it would," the largest of the goth set said, his white-blonde hair falling into his face when he shrugged. There was a gleam of excitement in his eyes, though.

"If it worked, why are there two of them?" The Black man narrowed his eyes at me. "And why is one of them not wearing shoes? Are those…ducklings on your socks?"

"Yes. To be fair, I got pulled from my bedroom, about to fall asleep," I pointed out. Then I shook my head. "No, wait. That's not important. What *is* important?"

I looked at Baz. He coughed and pointed to the circle we stood in. I straightened. "Right! What's going on?"

The female goth grinned, revealing teeth as preternaturally white as Yolanda's. I tried not to stare. "We summoned you. We summoned Death! It was in Jacques' old recipe book, from his great-grandmother or something, and it worked!"

I frowned. Looked at the circle. Indeed, the lines painted on the ground were the right sort for summoning. But both Death and Life were forbidden from answering summonings to the mortal realms, and these were definitely the mortal realms. Then I remembered that I now had Death's heart in my chest and groaned. I wasn't Death, but I was close enough that a summoning circle wouldn't be able to tell the difference. And since I wasn't banned from being summoned to the mortal realms, that meant any fool with a family recipe could call on me.

Something would have to be done about that. As soon as I got back to Elsewhere.

I reached for my phone so I could call up a ride home, only my pockets were empty. My phone was gone. I patted myself down, growing increasingly desperate, until I remembered that Yolanda had taken it from me before watching the movie, so I couldn't do something stupid, like post a selfie on social media.

I looked to Baz and he shrugged. Right. Since when did he remember to carry his phone?

Finally, I turned to the desperate goths. Tried to smile politely. "I do hate to be an inconvenience, but I am not Death."

"You're basically Death," Baz said.

"Not helping," I hissed. I smiled again. "I'm not Death. My name is Cal Thorpe, and while I *work* for Death, I am decidedly not he. Oh, and this is my cousin, Baz."

All eyes narrowed on me. There was some desperate muttering into various ears, as well as consulting a very old book that was falling apart and stained with something that looked a little like barbecue sauce. Or blood.

Then, from the cheerful female: "Well, if you work for Death, it will have to be good enough. You have been summoned and, therefore, are bound to our will until we release you."

"That's not how this works," I protested. "I'm bound to the *circle* until released, not to your will."

She deflated before my very eyes. "Oh. That doesn't mean you have to do what we say?"

Baz shrugged. "Sorry."

"Make a deal!" the Black man said, nodding eagerly. "If he works for Death, surely he can do what we need."

"Yeah!" This from the morose blonde. The other two, I realised, hadn't done anything but glower. I wondered if they could speak, or if they were even keen on what was going on here.

"Very well," the woman said, straightening. "I propose a deal, demon."

"Not a demon."

"You're not?" She looked disappointed when I shook my head. She looked again at my duckling socks and seemed to take that as proof I was telling the truth. "Oh. Still, you can help us!"

"With what, exactly?" I was wary, which was a good thing, given how unstable my emotions had been lately. Wariness was normal for me, as was grumpy discontent and generalised frustration with the world. All of which I was feeling at the moment.

"We need to break a curse." This revelation came from one of the two who had been previously silent, his brown-black hair slicked back, a studded dog collar at his neck.

"A curse?" Baz perked up in the most unhelpful manner.

"We're performing in one of the most important music festivals in the country, but everything has been going wrong, to the point where we're going to be dropped by the producers because of the bad press." The woman rubbed her neck. The other members of what I now realised was a band nodded in agreement.

"And how is that a curse?" I was a good marketing

agent, but perhaps these people were just bad musicians.

"Alice has almost been killed three times, Richard's best guitar was stolen, Bertie had his drum set relocated twice—once to the top of a hotel building—and I've had no less than three people try to mug me." The Black man was growling as he pointed to the woman, the dog-collared man, the morose blonde, and himself. That left the remaining silent man—large, his expression fixed in discontent, and with half his head shaved.

Baz nudged me. "This is good, Cal. A holiday! Solve a curse, help market the band, and have a good time while we're at it."

I scowled. "And your names?" I asked. "If they're Alice, Richard, and Bertie, you are—"

"Jacques and Steve," the Black man said. "Steve doesn't say much."

I heard a sharp intake of breath from Baz just as I put the puzzle pieces together. A band. The music that had been playing as Baz and I were summoned. A collection of goths, or rather, punks.

"Oh my—I know who you are!" Baz practically squealed.

"Oh, no," I breathed. Because I knew who they were, too.

Tiny Dinosaurs With Phasers, a punk band that had recently become stupidly popular in Elsewhere due to an accident of unfortunate proportions. Their music was generally considered terrible, but they were still massively well-known and loved. I, personally, had done my best to discourage this obsession. Every effort I'd made had failed. Spectacularly.

Now, in what was surely some revenge plot from Fate herself, they had summoned me to break a curse for them. And with Baz—perhaps their biggest fan— accidentally along for the ride, I knew that the next thing that came out of his mouth was going to be bad.

"We will absolutely help you!" Baz screamed.

Yep. Very, very bad.

CHAPTER 2

As one, the band members perked up, the taciturn Steve even going so far as to smile. Jacques reached out to shake Baz's hand, but was slapped away by Alice before he could cross the lines of the summoning circle and release us accidentally. I frowned, disappointed. That would have solved a lot of problems.

"Don't break the circle! We need to finalise the deal," Alice snapped. She smiled widely at us. "No offense."

"None taken," Baz said. "Cal is smart enough to get us out of just about any mess, and—"

I jabbed my cousin in the side with my elbow, feigning a polite smile. "How, exactly, would you like us to help you?"

"We want you to break the curse," Alice said.

"And make sure we stay in the music festival," Richard added, tugging at his earlobe. "We have to have a decent chance at this thing. The promo opportunities alone are worth a fortune."

I wasn't about to tell him that their music was a sensation in Elsewhere, no promotion required. Jacques made a face. "I don't suppose there's some way you could make us more popular. A spell or something?"

I tugged at the sleeves of my jumper and sniffed. "No. And even if there were, it would be cheating."

Baz nodded, still looking ridiculously cheerful. "Not that you guys need it. Really, you're awesome! I mean, all those nights in the bar, I would put on your first album and—"

I jabbed Baz in the side again. He'd been working at a magical bar when I had appeared back into his life— I'd been declared dead, due to my contract with Death, and it got very complicated, especially with my mother. I didn't want the band to know that his interference was likely what had their numbers soaring in Else-where; the number of customers who must have heard that drivel on repeat for years was terrifying.

"Worked in a bar?" Bertie looked confused. "I thought you were an assistant to Death."

"That would be me," I said. "Baz is my cousin. And, ah, the manifestation of Justice, a career he took *after* working at a bar."

Just in case these people decided they wanted to pursue cheating.

"Right," Jacques said. He didn't look particularly convinced, but then I *was* wearing socks with baby ducks on it, which wasn't exactly what people associated with Death. Though, what they expected with a poorly painted summoning circle from a recipe found in a book covered in barbecue sauce, I couldn't say. "You can do what we ask, can't you?"

I shrugged and shoved my glasses up my nose. "I mean, I'm no expert in curses, but I should be able to figure out who would want to curse you, at least. Do some investigation. Actually stopping the curse might require outside services, but I will do my best."

This answer did not seem to appease them. The band members talked amongst themselves in low voices, but I got the impression that I wasn't quite what they wanted.

Well, if you try to summon Death in a shop with an articulated chicken skeleton, right around bed time, then you get what you get. I could feel my expression slipping into a scowl; a full-blown litany of complaints was building, and there was no popcorn or coffee to calm me down.

"Are you sure you work for Death?" Alice finally asked, looking me over uncertainly.

"I do," I said firmly. "I'm his, ah…" I did *not* want to tell these people that I was his marketing agent. That would require actually using my prodigious skills in that area to help the band, and while I was perfectly content to do work for the many, many dwarven princes and princesses, or the sellers of coffee, or other such things, the thought of marketing a band whose music I detested—though their brand clothing was very comfortable—did not appeal. I smiled and nodded my head. "I'm Death's assistant."

The second heart beating in my chest fluttered for a second, as if laughing at my obfuscation. It was close enough. Right?

Baz shot me a look I could feel even behind his sunglasses, but let the matter lie. Finally, their uncertainty still plain, the band members nodded and Jacques reached across the lines of the summoning circle to shake my hand. That wasn't really how these things worked; they were supposed to get me to agree before breaking the circle, but I would make allowances for naïveté. Besides, I needed to borrow a phone so I could contact the office and tell them not to expect me for a day or two.

Or three.

I desperately hoped it wasn't more than three.

I shook Jacques' hand. A bargain was struck.

"Right," I said, stepping over the lines on the ground. "First things first."

"Shoes?" Bertie suggested. I wiggled my toes in my socks and sighed.

"I don't suppose you have Italian leather?"

—

As it turned out, they did not have Italian leather shoes. Instead, I found myself walking through an antiques shop wearing fluffy bunny slippers borrowed from Jacques' uncle, who owned the place. When asked why they did a summoning circle in an antiques shop, the band hemmed and hawwed until finally Richard admitted that they wanted to be surrounded by as much death-related stuff as they could, and antiques were old enough to be death-related.

Somehow, their logic—ill-founded and ridiculous as it might be, given that summoning circles worked anywhere—made sense to me.

The bunny slippers, however, were so horrendous as to keep my mouth shut on the minor compliment.

I borrowed Steve's phone, called up Agravane, and explained the situation. While he laughed to the point of tears, I relayed instructions for the office in my absence. Agravane promised he would have Yolanda send a messenger pixie with my phone and wallet within the hour and then asked if he could share the story on social media. I told him off in no uncertain terms.

Then, primly hanging up, I realised I forgot to tell him a message for Neja, and wondered if the messenger pixie would be here soon. I handed Steve back his phone; he took it with two fingers and held it out, as if I'd turned into a vile demon. I supposed the bunny slippers and ducky socks weren't enough to make him believe I was a reasonable chap.

That upset me more than it should, and I found myself close to tears as I mulled over a mismatched tea set by the window. Baz came up to me and patted me on the shoulder. "There, there. The band, you know, they're artistic sorts. Not used to working with someone so…so…" he trailed off.

My tears dissipated and I found my usual grumpy mood returning. I hated to admit, but maybe he'd been right about this holiday thing. After a month of fluctuating emotions, I was feeling much more myself and had only been away from Elsewhere for twenty minutes. Then, I glanced out the window and was certain that I was closer to normal than I'd been in a very long time.

Why?

Because, the sight that met me? It brought up frustration and disappointment, a hint of anger, and a general dissatisfaction with the way things were working out. Exactly what I normally felt on a bad day. As this was apparently turning out to be.

"Cal?" Baz asked, noting my change in expression. "What's wrong? Do we need to call Agravane back? Maybe have Yolanda come in person? Do I need to get Neja?"

"No," I groused. "It's fine. Just…" I gestured vaguely at the sight outside the window. There were tall buildings as far as the eye could see, with concrete and a few stunted trees studding the footpath outside the buildings. There were cars everywhere. People walking the streets, hands shoved into pockets and heads down. It was a city, much like any large city. Only, I recognised this one. I'd been here before.

Chicago.

The last time I'd been here, I was carrying around Al Capone's soul, and was on loan from Death to his cousin, the Taxman. Things had, as one would expect, gone tragically wrong, and I found myself in a vast number of fatal and uncomfortable circumstances. Oh, and the FBI were involved.

Needless to say, Chicago was not my favourite city in the world.

Baz looked confused. I brought my shoulders to my ears and shuddered. "Let's just say that Chicago and I have a very poor relationship."

"Chicago? As in the place Neja and you first met? When she dropped a piano on you?" Baz seemed a little too pleased with that information.

"I would ask how you know that story, but as Agravane is a notorious gossip, there isn't much point. Hopefully, there will be no pianos falling on me *this* time around." Given that I was now working closely with a bunch of musicians who were attending a music festival with a bunch of other musicians, my chances were not impossible. With that depressing thought, I turned away from the window.

"Alright, since we're waiting on the messenger pixie for my phone and such, we might as well get started," I informed the band. They all straightened, looking ready for some sort of miracle or magic or the like. I didn't want to disappoint them, but I performed no such things. At least, not intentionally. I pointed at Alice. "When did all of this begin?"

"Three days ago," she said, nodding firmly. Her nose scrunched, the silver stud there catching in the light. "Well, three and a half, because it really started Saturday night, and today is Tuesday."

"And how did it start?" Baz asked, folding his arms. He sounded a bit too much like a cop from one of Yolanda's soap operas. Obviously, my cousin and my assistant had been spending too much time together.

Richard frowned, scratching his chin. "My guitar was stolen."

Bertie rolled his eyes. "It wasn't stolen. It went missing from the gear and reappeared hanging from the catwalk with all its strings cut. Security cameras prove that none of the roadies did it, or any of the other bands."

"Camera footage can be forged," I pointed out.

"Nah, not this stuff. It's *oooollllddd*," Alice said. "They still use tapes!"

Baz and I exchanged a look. Surely we weren't that old, but I still remembered the use of tapes. And Baz, being my age, would remember the same thing. I would have thought Alice and her bandmates our contemporaries, but that was obviously wrong. Suddenly, I was feeling grumpier than usual.

"Tapes can be forged. Anyways," Baz said, looking at me. "What happened next?"

"We went to dinner, and coming out of the restaurant, Alice nearly got run over by a car, a vespa, and some kid on a skateboard. In that order." Jacques looked angry at this, his mouth tight, chin raised. Somehow, I thought that the threat of bodily harm bothered him more than the potential damage of some instruments. I began to like him a bit more.

"And my drums!" Bertie said. "They were relocated. Three times!"

I nodded. "Well, all of that is annoying—and even dangerous, I will grant you—but it hardly sounds like a curse."

Here, they winced. As one. Which wasn't suspicious at all.

Finally, Richard nodded to Steve, who was scowling at the floor. "Well, you see, Steve here is a witch. Passed down through his mother's side. He says that we're surrounded with a...a...what did you call it?"

"Miasma," Steve said, grumbling the one word so quietly I could barely hear.

"Yeah, that." Richard cleared his throat. "Apparently, it gets worse when we're at the festival. And Steve says that he can feel it when things are about to go wrong. And that it's getting worse."

"You believe him?" Baz asked. Most people would have included a note of incredulity in their voice at the receipt of such information, but most people hadn't had actual encounters with such beings as Life and Death and Fae and rock trolls and talking cats and djinns. Witches were more on the commonplace end of the magical scale for Baz and me. Either way, Steve bristled at Baz, scowling harder at my cousin than at the floor. Even *I* felt the animosity coming from that look, and I was generally immune to glares and scowls.

"They did summon us, after all," I said in a dry voice. "I imagine that rather proves beyond a reasonable doubt the existence of magic. So the question isn't whether they believe that Steve here is a witch, but who placed the curse."

Steve's glare subsided, and he went back to studying the floor tiles.

"Alright, so you're cursed. Are you the only ones?" I asked. "Any other miasmas at the music festival?"

Jacques shrugged. "A couple other bands have been having some difficulties. Space Jumpship blew out an entire stage's speakers when they plugged in an amp wrong."

"Oh, yeah! And there was the incident with The Office Supplies getting food poisoning, even though a bunch of other people ate the same stuff." Alice nodded. She froze, her face suddenly going pale. "You don't think someone is trying to sabotage the *music festival*, do you?"

I shrugged. "I'm not very good with these sorts of things, so I don't know. But it's possible."

I should have been asking more questions, like who could want to sabotage the music festival, which bands were being targeted, why Tiny Dinosaurs might consider themselves the target of a curse, but frankly, I was beginning to care more about where my phone was than the fate of the festival.

"We need a plan," Baz said, nudging me with his elbow. I straightened my shoulders and tried to pay better attention. "We'll start with a tour of the festival grounds, maybe see if we can spot anything odd. And then we can see if there's a way to break the curse, or at least keep people from being seriously hurt."

"How many bands are performing at this festival?" I asked.

"Seventy two," Jacques said. "All different genres. It's huge."

Marvellous. Seventy-two potential suspects. Well, sixty-nine, if you took away Tiny Dinosaurs, The Office Supplies, and Space Jumpship. What was with band names these days? Shaking my head, I tried not to say anything snarky, which was a huge mark of restraint for me. Then, before I could offer a more specific plan of attack—one that included a shoe shop —there was a *thud* against the window and Steve let out a bloodcurdling shriek.

"Ah," Baz said cheerfully. "That'll be the messenger pixie!"

CHAPTER 3

Once the messenger pixie had been dusted off and paid—with every band mate including Silent Steve staring openly—I checked my phone for any messages, futzed with a couple of social media posts, sent a quick explanatory text to my girlfriend, and we were on our way. I, regretfully, wore the bunny slippers, having decided that they were the lesser of evils to going sock-footed through the streets of Chicago. Alas, the band almost immediately forgot about my desire for proper shoes and instead had us piling into a van and driving off to the venue for the festival.

Now, I am the sort of person that prefers classical music, or even a nice jazz, and so have not been to any music festivals before. My cousin, on the other hand, has spent a great deal of time in a number of unsavoury places in the name of entertainment, and so was able to fill me in. Essentially, he said that the bands for the festival were all here for set-up and rehearsal. Some showed up a week before the start of the festival, others only hours before, depending on the importance of the band. Tiny Dinosaurs with Phasers, being a small punk band with a cultish following—except in Elsewhere—and therefore of no real significance, had arrived the full week early.

We thus had two days before the festival really started. During that time, Baz and I would wander the festival and try to determine the source of the curse. I'd been furiously texting with Agravane about how to find and nullify curses, since Neja wasn't answering my messages, being busy. Agravane was unhelpful, claiming that he had no idea and hoped that I would have fun. I threatened to promote him, which resulted only in radio silence.

Having employees is such a pain, sometimes.

"Well?" Baz asked while Bertie drove through a traffic light with an increase of acceleration that was terrifying, even for someone who couldn't die. "Any luck?"

"We're on our own," I grumbled. "Yolanda said she'd talk to Death about the summoning circle situation, Agravane basically told us to figure it out, and Neja sent a pre-written reply of, 'Sorry! Off to the Northern Wastes. Be back in a week.' So, unless you know someone else I can ask, then we're on our own."

"My grandmother is good with curses," Jacques offered. "It was her recipe book where we got the summoning spell."

"If your grandmother is so good with curses, then why didn't you call her before, oh, I don't know, attempting to make a deal with Death?" I snapped. The air in the van suddenly got very thick, and no one in the band would look at me. Silence prevailed. Baz snickered.

"They bypassed the family members and went straight for you, dear cousin. You should be flattered!" Baz smacked me on the shoulder. I wanted to throttle him, the thought coming on me with a surge of rage so blinding that I literally lost track of my surroundings for a moment. When things resolved themselves, my hands were already in the air, reaching for Baz's neck. He squeaked, pulling back as far as possible—which in a transit van that had seven people in it, was not far.

I lowered my hands. "Well, I suppose I'm not quite myself yet, still."

"You think?" Baz asked, voice still high. "Next time you have an emotional breakdown, could you *not* go straight to murderous?"

"I'll do my best," I replied drily. Turning back to Jacques, who was watching all of this with slack-jawed confusion, I asked, "Where is your grandmother, and how, exactly, can I get hold of her?"

"There's really no need to get my grandmother involved," Jacques said. He started wringing his hands, looking decidedly uncomfortable. "She's a bit intense, can be very loud. You know? And she doesn't even like the music, so I don't really invite her to band events and—"

"Do you want the curse broken or not?" I asked. Jacques winced. Alice nudged him with her shoulder.

"Come on, man," she hissed in a half-hearted

attempt at a whisper. "How bad can it be? Don't forget, we hired my dad as a roadie last year. Your grandmother can't be worse than that!"

The saxophonist hunched his shoulders, rubbing the back of his neck. I waited, glaring at the bunny slippers on my feet. Something in my expression must have made clear the direness of the situation, either that or Baz's encouraging smiles tipped the scales. Either way, Jacques nodded and grumbled, then pulled out his phone and dialed a number.

"Hi, Nona?" he said. "Yes, it's me, Jacques…well, no, I haven't gotten myself arrested…no, no one's dead… yes, Nona, I passed on your message to Mom…well, that's sort of why I'm calling. You remember that recipe book you gave me? Yes, that one. Well, the band and I, we sort of used that spell you said we shouldn't use. And, well, it worked."

Suddenly, Jacques held the phone away from his ear, wincing. A very angry woman's voice sounded through the speaker, words running together too quickly for me to hear. She had the musical tone of a banshee, and judging by the way everyone else held their ears, I wasn't the only one who thought so. Finally, the yelling subsided, and Jacques held the phone to his ear again.

"Yes, Nona, I'm sorry. I won't do it again. Only, well, the band and I…yes, Nona, we're in trouble. Cursed. No, it wasn't Alice! See, the thing is…no…it's only… Nona! Will you let me speak? Thank you. Yes, I'm sorry for shouting. The thing is, the guy we summoned, he isn't actually Death, but his assistant, and well, he doesn't actually specialise in curses. Yes, he needs help. No, I haven't signed away my soul. No, none of the band has signed away their souls either. No, not even Alice…We're in Chicago. Yes, I know, I should have visited earlier. Sorry, Nona, I was busy with band stuff and…you can meet us at the music festival if you want. I'll be sure there's a pass waiting for you at the front gate. Yes, thank you, Nona. I love you too."

With a click and a sigh of relief, Jacques lowered his phone and leaned his head back on his seat. "She'll help."

"Great!" Baz said. "So, when do we get to this venue?"

"We're there," Bertie announced, pulling roughly into a parking space that was definitely designed for a much smaller vehicle. The various members of the band piled out of the car and stretched their limbs eagerly. I grumbled, still wearing bunny slippers. Baz, at least, was ridiculously cheerful, snatching my phone so he could take a picture of himself at the festival. I stole my phone back and shoved it into my pocket, all but snarling at him.

"Somebody hasn't had enough coffee this morning." Baz was altogether too cheerful. I wondered if he would be less smiley if I decked him across the jaw. Rationally, I knew that wasn't a normal thing to wonder, and so managed to keep my hands in my pockets—barely. None of the band members seemed to notice my mood, except perhaps Steve, who took a healthy step away from me as soon as he could. He said nothing, just eyeing me and moving farther away.

Alice, meanwhile, threaded her arm through Baz's, pointing out the sights.

As far as I could tell, the venue that housed the music festival was nothing more than a large park with an amphitheatre built in and several temporary stages set up. It looked like there were enough spaces for seven or eight bands to play at one time, and still have room for vendors and food trucks. A big place, certainly, but nothing magical. Not so far as I could tell, at least.

At this time of the morning—that is, nearly seven according to my phone—there weren't many people about at all. A few techs lugging sound equipment, one or two cleaners sweeping up napkins and the like, a couple of vendors setting up booths. Mostly, the people wandering around had the look of security. That is, they were larger than average, had bigger shoes than average, and were swiftly avoided by everyone else.

"We'll get you in the gate and you can start having a look around," Jacques promised Baz and I. We approached the gate and found it manned with not one, not two, but three security officers. That seemed excessive for this time of morning, even to me. Baz shot me a look over his shoulder, one that echoed my own thoughts on the matter. Something was up.

As the band gathered in front of the gate, showing passes and ID, the thought that something was up became fact. From behind the ticket booth stepped a woman. One I knew. Average height, strong build, firm expression, hair maybe a little more silver than I'd seen before, frown a little more ingrained. She looked over the band with a skeptical eye, then paused as she came to my bunny slippers.

With a long, drawn out look, she took in every inch of me, from the slippers to the ducky socks that peeked over top, the pressed trousers in a shade of midnight blue, the jumper a complimentary red, finally stopping when she met my gaze. Then, because of course she did, she grinned at me.

Of all the people I had to run into while visiting Chicago, it had to be the only one I knew.

"Well, well, well," Agent Ferris of the FBI said, propping her hands on her hips and very blatantly showing off her gun and badge to me. "If it isn't Cal Thorpe! The last time I saw you, you were working for the IRS? And now look at you! Moonlight as, what, a comedic act?"

"The tax consultant position was a temporary posting," I muttered. "And if you're referring to the slippers—"

"Oh, I most certainly am."

"—Then I would inform you that my regular shoes were…damaged. Are you going to suspect a man based on his footwear, Agent Ferris?" I was starting to get that murdery feeling again.

"No, of course not. I only think that it seems suspicious, all these strange events happening at the Chicagoland Music Festival. And then *you* show up, someone around whom strange events are all but guaranteed to happen."

"Hey!" I protested. "That's a false correlation! The events happen *first* and then I have to fix it."

"I like her," Baz whispered in my ear. "Care to introduce us?"

I jumped, nearly screaming at the touch of Baz's breath on my ear. "Can you *not* sneak up on me right now?" I demanded.

Agent Ferris raised a single brow. Her expression grew more amused and somehow more suspicious at the same time. A quite impressive feat, actually. I took three deep breaths, smoothed down my jumper, and proceeded to the introductions.

"Agent Ferris, may I introduce to you my cousin, Basil Thorpe, also known as Baz. Baz, this is Agent… ah, I don't think I've ever learned your first name." The last time we'd met, she had been chasing down the fetch-slash-mobster Dermot Green for various illegal activities, while I had been also chasing him down for refusal to pay back taxes. There had been drama, and being possessed by Al Capone, and definitely a lot of me dying, but we'd ended on a reasonably civil note. Of course, in the middle of all the palaver, I hadn't ever learned her full name.

"Sophia," she said. "And it's Special Agent Ferris, now, Mr. Thorpe."

"Really? Congratulations on the promotion. Anyways, Baz, meet Special Agent Sophia Ferris. Oh, and surely you know the band Tiny Dinosaurs with Phasers." I waved dismissively at the band members, who were all staring at me as though I'd grown a second head. Claim to be the assistant for Death and get normal conversation. Know an FBI agent by name and suddenly I'm some terrifying creature. Figures.

Ferris frowned at the band, scrutinising them with the sort of care one generally takes for criminals. Frankly, I wasn't sure any of these musicians had the subtlety for criminal enterprise. Eventually, Ferris nodded. "Punk band. Terrible music, comfortable clothes. Yes, I'm familiar."

Oddly, none of the band seemed chagrined by that description, though Steve did kick at the ground with his metal toed boots. Jacques sighed. "Yeah, our merchandise vendor is very capable. Our merch sales outnumber our album sales by three, at least. It's a bit weird."

"So, Special Agent Ferris," Baz said, peering over the edges of his sunglasses at her, "what exactly are you doing here?"

Maybe it was the fact that he was Justice embodied, or perhaps it was just the fact that people—almost universally—got along with Baz, but she answered almost immediately. "There have been some unusual happenings at the festival. Instruments mangled, stolen, or moved. People reporting ill or injured. Nothing major, but enough to raise suspicions of, ah, ill-intent."

"And since when does the FBI investigate a music festival?" Alice snapped. Ferris' eyes hardened and her jaw twitched as she rested her hand on her hip, inches from her gun.

"Let's try not to antagonise law enforcement," I said, though Alice only glared. Turning to Ferris, I couldn't help but wonder the same thing. "She does have a point, Special Agent. It seems odd that the FBI would send someone as important as you to what is basically a bunch of music nerds wandering around with bad food for several hours a day."

As one, the band bristled. Bertie even went so far as to take a step towards me, which I discouraged with a single quirk of my brow. He must have remembered who he was dealing with—slippers aside—and decided that discretion was the better part of valour. Either that, or he was just surprisingly intelligent. I was willing to bet good coffee that it was the former.

"It is not my duty to inform potential suspects why they are being investigated at this juncture. Needless to say, festivals such as these are often far more than they seem. Especially since you are here, Mr. Thorpe. This is, what, your third official run-in with law enforcement recently? Impersonating an Interpol officer—"

"Those credentials were valid," I protested. They were absolutely not valid.

"Working as a tax collections agent for the IRS," Ferris continued. "And now, what, you're an image consultant for a punk band?"

"Nothing quite so glamorous, I assure you," I quipped. Image consultant indeed. The Tiny Dinosaurs members needed far more than my expertise if they were to improve their image. Oh, I will grant you that I'm quite capable as a marketer, but even I have my limits.

"Then what?" Agent Ferris asked. She stared me down, and I was absolutely certain that this situation would end right here, with me being denied entry to the park and therefore unable to do my job. Baz would never let me live this down, but thankfully, I was perfectly alright with going back to my job in Elsewhere and leaving this debacle be.

Only, as per usual, things didn't go according to plan.

Before I could give Special Agent Ferris a reasonable explanation for why I was there—one that she would believe given my unusual history with her—a noise like the bellow of an elephant drew our attention. The sound bellowed again, and a moment later a car the size of a small yacht pulled up to the curb with a squeal of breaks and a pop. It was black, shined up and gleaming, and an absolute monstrosity. The person who climbed out, though, seemed like she could handle it.

She was tiny, Black, and had a shock of white hair so bright that it reflected the sun. She looked to be maybe eighty, though her skin was exceptionally smooth. She wore a blue jumpsuit with the name *Imogen* embroidered on the breast, a pair of glasses so thick that they magnified her eyes a thousand fold, and clutched what looked like a picnic basket.

"Yoo-hoo!" she said, and immediately I recognised the voice as belonging to Jacques' grandmother. Slightly accented with a French-Creole tone, her voice carried exceptionally well. "Jacques Girard! Now, don't you worry, I brought all my curse-breaking equipment. Where's the demon I'm meant to be working with?"

As one, the band pointed to me.

Agent Ferris burst out laughing. "Oh, I can't wait to hear the explanation for this one!"

gent Ferris worked her magic and the band was let inside. They immediately scarpered off to their stage for a sound check while Baz, Jacques' nona, Agent Ferris and I followed a little more slowly. Ferris was silent, obviously waiting for an explanation. Unfortunately for her, Jacques' nona hadn't stopped talking since she arrived.

"Oh, it is just so nice to meet you! I'm Valerie, Jacques' grandmother, who he doesn't call nearly enough, despite being in the same city. Pah! This band of his takes up too much of his time. Did you know that he plays the saxophone good enough to be in the New York Symphony? Oh, yes! Played two seasons and then quit, just so he could go gallivanting off with that ridiculous band of his, Tiny Birds or whatever. And now look at him! Stuck under a curse! What am I going to do—"

"Ma'am," Agent Ferris said at last, drawing us all

over to a picnic table. The band was setting up not too far from us, and I watched them with casual interest, more so I could catch any strange doings than because I cared about a sound check. "Please, if we could just straighten this out."

"Of course!" Valerie said, patting Agent Ferris' hand. "Now, let me see. My grandson called and said that he was trying to break a curse that had been put on his band. I'm something of an aficionado for magic, you see. My great, great-grandmother was a striga. Italian. Set my poor French great, great-grandfather into fits over her particular talents. Oh, the arguments! Right, yes, anyways, I could easily help with the curse, but my grandson said he had already summoned, ah, well, the recipe is for summoning Death, but apparently it didn't work, because all it got was Death's assistant. I must say, boy, you don't look much like a demon."

"Because I'm not," I said. I didn't point out the fact that I was a Reaper, nor that I carried Death's heart beating in my chest beside my own. I was—at least, I still believed myself to be—human.

I eyed Agent Ferris, waiting for some announcement of my being insane, but she seemed perfectly calm. "I'm not going to scream, if that's what you're waiting for," she said evenly. "I remember the night of the car accident, even if you pretend not to."

I winced. That was right in the middle of the Al Capone Crisis, as I liked to call my last trip to Chicago, and Agent Ferris had accidentally got caught up in a death wish I'd been put under. Of course, seeing as I couldn't die, it didn't end well. She'd had a broken leg, I was killed. It was more than a little dramatic.

"Go on, Cal, just tell her. Valerie won't care, and frankly, I'm curious to see what the good Agent does with this information," Baz said, a peculiar expression on his face. He was studying the FBI agent with a great deal of scrutiny, even given the sunglasses. Something about his Justice role must have been piqued by Ferris. I didn't even want to think what that might mean for my time here in Chicago.

"Very well," I said, folding my hands on the table. Valerie leaned forwards with wide-eyed interest, and even Ferris was paying strict attention. "As you might have guessed, Special Agent Ferris, I am not actually a tax accountant."

"Really?" she drawled. To Valerie's confusion, she explained, "He was pretending to be a tax accountant the last time we met. He was really quite bad at it."

I scowled. "I was *on loan* to the Taxman. It was temporary! Just because he's Death's cousin and—"

"Wait, you mean you do actually claim to work for Death?" Ferris asked, suddenly deadly serious.

"Yes, of course." I sniffed disdainfully. The band was busy hauling speakers about, apparently too low down the hierarchy to rate help from the roadies. "I was hired on by Death to be his marketing agent. Since then, I've taken on more, ah, tasks and duties. So when the band attempted to summon Death—which can't actually be done here in the mortal realms, by the way, so you should probably update your recipe book, Valerie— they got me instead."

"I thought Death only worked with demons." Valerie sounded disappointed.

"I'm human. Born and raised in London. I just happened to have a particular talent that Death needed, is all, so when I died, he hired me." Ah, yes, getting shot in the park. Good times.

"Well, that's alright then." Valerie patted my hand. "It explains your lack of experience with curses and the like. Don't you worry, I'll teach you everything you need to know."

"You can't be serious!" Ferris said, aghast. "You can't actually believe him!"

There it was, the logical FBI agent showing through, refusing to believe in the supernatural. I sighed.

"Why not?" Valerie shrugged. "He seems nice enough."

"And you!" Ferris jabbed a finger at Baz, who smiled his best charming smile. "What exactly is *your* role in all of this nonsense?"

Baz took Ferris' hand and kissed it. "I, dear lady, am Cal's recalcitrant cousin. I am also, as it happens, Justice."

She burst out laughing.

Baz looked offended, reaching up to adjust his sunglasses as he frowned at the picnic table. Valerie made to pat him on the shoulder, then looked at me and shrugged, as if to say that not everyone was as reasonable as she was. I had to agree.

I was about to suggest something crazy, like we go and prove my claims—I have no doubt Ferris wouldn't mind shooting me, especially if she knew I'd come back —when there was a shout from the stage. Alice, holding a microphone stand like a sword, was waving it about furiously while some sort of flying creature dove at her.

As one, the four of us on the investigative side of things rose and started for the stage.

"Get it away from me!" Alice shrieked, immediately demonstrating why she was the singer. Bertie threw a drum stick at the creature, and even a couple of roadies and a sound engineer carrying a tablet computer had come to see what the trouble was. The rest of the band was unhelpfully gawking.

As we drew closer, I saw what, exactly, was attacking Alice. It was a bat. Not a little brown bat, like we had in England, nor one of the smaller American types. It was massive, with teeth big enough that I could see them from twenty feet away. Frankly, given that and the orange tinge to the eyes, I was convinced this wasn't a bat normally found in the mortal realms. Something had brought it here, and now it was flying about in the middle of the day in Chicago.

"Do something!" Ferris snarled at me.

"Me?" I was hardly qualified for animal control. "What about you?!"

"What do you want me to do, shoot it?" she demanded. I thought that was a good idea, but apparently she didn't. Instead, we both glared at each other for a moment before Valerie stepped between us and set her picnic basket down. She opened the lid, pulled out several jars with dried herbs in them, and then rustled about a bit before finally extracting a net.

Not just any net.

A golden net.

Before any of us could do anything, this eighty-year-old woman stepped forwards, flinging the gold net high enough into the air that it snagged the bat with ease. The creature let out an indignant squawk which was definitely not a normal bat noise, then plummeted to the stage, completely tangled.

Alice managed to let out one more shriek before passing out entirely. Steve, thankfully, caught her.

We all drew closer to the bat, still wriggling and struggling in the net. It was most definitely not a normal bat, with its purple-veined wings so dark they were almost black, spikes along the back of its head, and claws that dripped with some sort of oozing liquid. Poison, most likely. The golden net seemed to subdue the creature neatly; it just stared at us with its orange eyes, barely containing the obvious fury it felt.

"Poor thing," Valerie crooned. "You're very far from home, aren't you?"

"Why did the gold net work?" Baz asked. "Why do you even have a gold net?"

"Gold is a good conductor," Valerie said, "and when it comes to magical energies, this one is bound with a containment spell. Very trick to break on its own, and amplified by the gold. Family heirloom. First time I've used it! Gosh, wasn't that fun!"

"What *is* that thing?" Ferris had one hand resting on her gun, and she looked a bit pale. Her eyes flicked to mine and I saw something there that would have been fear in a normal person. In Agent Ferris, I thought it might be realisation, specifically the realisation that as much as she might want, things weren't as she had thought. I felt badly for her; it wasn't easy to have your worldview ripped out from beneath you, even with a prior encounter with me.

"Are you alright?" Baz asked Ferris, with more than a little concern colouring his tone. There was definitely some sort of strangeness with him regarding the FBI agent. A pull, perhaps, in his capacity as Justice.

Ferris just hunched her shoulders and stared at the bat. "Fine," she snapped. "Just…get rid of whatever that *thing* is."

"Looks Fae," I said, nudging the bat with one of my bunny slippers. It hissed and tried to sink its fangs into the ear of the slipper, missing only by millimetres. I yelped, stepped backwards, and promptly fell off the stage. My entire body felt the impact with the ground, even if it was only a few feet down. My muscles screamed, I'm fairly certain I herniated a disc in my back, and also I managed to hit my head, judging by the large pool of blood by my ear.

"Cal?" Baz asked. "You okay?"

"Just kill me now," I grumbled, only half-joking. One of my "deaths" usually managed to clear up any injuries with ease. It was preferable to bleeding everywhere.

"I'll call a medic," Ferris said, sounding as though she were glad of an excuse to get away from us for a moment. In the mean time, Valerie kept humming over the bat, entirely unconcerned with my injured state.

"What do we do with it?" she asked. "I don't have room in my picnic basket."

"Find a container for it, and we'll release it across the nearest veil to Faerie this evening," I suggested, still prone on the ground. "There's usually one or two in most major mortal cities. Fae are the most common ones to cross over."

And travelling through Faerie was a nightmare of politics and social manoeuvrings, which is why I tried my best to avoid it. That, and I'd almost started a war and then ended it in the very same trip. The Winter Court still hadn't forgiven me.

"How exactly are we meant to find a veil to Faerie?" Ferris asked, as though I were suggesting something incredibly stupid.

"I deal in curses, not the Fae," Valerie said. "I wonder if Jacques' saxophone case is big enough for the bat…"

I groaned and sat up, my entire spine screaming in protest. After determining that I was, unfortunately, still bleeding from my head, I decided against further movement. Baz handed me a paper towel.

"The easiest way is to go around loudly proclaiming a desire for some ridiculous dream. Like, 'I'd sell my soul for a mansion' or something," Baz said with a shrug. "They'll congregate like bees." I winced up at him, holding the paper towel to my throbbing skull.

"Since when do you deal with the Fae?"

Baz shuddered. "Since an incident involving court

politics and a demand for justice. My goodness, those people are insane! Oh, by the way, a very angry cat named Shakespeare told me to tell you that one day, he would kill you."

Death's former pet, a grimalkin, had it out for me after I'd revealed—and foiled—his plan for war. He hated me. The feeling was mutual.

"It's like I've walked onto the set of some magical stage play, only no one knows their lines and the actors are all insane." Ferris wandered off to the edge of the stage, perhaps to go call those medics, while Valerie wrestled the angry bat into what looked like a speaker case.

"You okay?" Baz asked. I shrugged.

"Ruined another jumper. And these shoes are *hideous*." My voice came out despondent, tearful even, and I was on the point of breaking out in great, gasping sobs as I had done when we were out of popcorn.

"There, there." Baz patted my shoulder, the one not currently getting bled on my a head wound. "Let's get the band sorted, and then maybe you can get Valerie to give you a ride to a mall or something."

I sniffled and nodded, blowing my nose on the bloody paper towels and then immediately feeling disgusted by that. I let out a squeal of dismay, tossed the paper towel into the air, where it was promptly swept up by a pigeon and carried away.

I gaped after the bird. Baz gaped after the bird. Even Valerie, mid-bat wrangling, gaped after the bird.

"Cal?" Baz asked.

"Uh-huh?"

"Did that pigeon just fly away with a sample of your blood?"

"Uh-huh."

"That's bad, isn't it?"

"Uh-huh."

Why couldn't my life ever be easy?

CHAPTER 5

Several hours later, after I'd been given a cursory check over by the medics—who looked at me askance after checking my pulse, one of the downsides of having two hearts—and been fed, provided with new clothes and shoes thanks to the magic of the gig economy and hiring personal shoppers, I met with Tiny Dinosaurs and Company in their hotel.

It was a very sad hotel. There were shifty eyed plants in the lobby, and when we congregated in Alice's room, I was certain we were breaking fire code by having nine people there. Not to mention I thought I heard mice in the walls. At least, I hope they were mice.

I tried not to look too closely at the stains on the bathroom wall, but I'm fairly certain it was blood splatter. A lot of blood splatter. I shuddered when Alice and Bertie sat on one of the two double beds. They seemed unconcerned. Baz, also, sat in the single chair in the room without a qualm. Ferris winced when he did, exchanging a glance and a shudder with me.

Valerie, at least, pulled out what looked like a bath towel from her picnic basket and spread it on the other bed before she sat. The rest of us stood, trying to point-edly ignore the furious noises coming from the speaker cabinet where the faerie bat was stored.

"So," Baz said as I tried not to hyperventilate at the amount of dust in the room.

"You believe us about the curse, now, don't you?" Alice blurted.

"I never doubted there was a curse, but I am partic-ularly annoyed that it involves the Fae."

"Like fairies, right?" Ferris asked. "Pixies and Peter Pan and the like? I can't believe I'm actually asking that question. How the hell am I going to write up this report?"

I doubted that writing up a report was really her top priority, but regarding coping mechanisms, it was to each their own. I tended towards snark. Ferris, apparently, worried about paperwork.

"Think more along the lines of Scottish and Irish spirits who prey on children, have a pathological dislike of iron, tell the truth. Tricky sorts," Baz said. He scowled in the direction of the bat. "Have a whole arsenal of nasty creatures to do their bidding, also."

"Pah!" Valerie said. "They're just people. Magical ones. But they can be stopped. A curse always has a means of breaking it."

What concerned me was that whoever had brought this curse down upon the music festival was dealing with the Fae at all. They were vengeful, often blood-thirsty, and very good at loopholes. That, and the last time I'd dealt with the Fae, I'd really pissed them off. It occurred to me that I managed to piss off a lot of people in the normal course of my life. Not that my life was anything remotely approaching normal.

"Cal?" Ferris asked, crossing her arms. "*Can* it be broken?"

I shrugged. "In all likelihood, yes. Whoever did this wasn't using a spell themselves, but probably made a deal with a Faerie, or a group of Fae, or something, who are then wreaking havoc at their behest. It would almost be easier if it were just a spell."

"Spells can be broken," Valerie said helpfully. Steve nodded in agreement, though I noted he didn't add anything helpful, despite being a witch. Perhaps the Fae were out of his comfort zone.

"Spells can," I said. "Faeries must be outsmarted. Or killed. Which is annoyingly difficult, given that they're semi-immortal."

Ferris scoffed. "Semi-immortal? No such thing."

"Special Agent, may I remind you that you're working with an employee of Death?" Jacques gestured at me, his grandmother nodding her head.

"Him?" Ferris frowned. The last time we'd spent any time together, I'd had to shield her from being crushed by a car when a light post fell on it. I'd walked away unscathed—died a bit, though. She ended up with a broken leg. I could see she was remembering too, because she was shifting her weight, hand resting on her hip above her gun. "He's just resilient."

I see we were back in denial territory with the illustrious FBI agent. I would probably have to die right in front of her for her to believe that I was in any way associated with Death. And, despite the splitting headache from falling off the stage, I was in no mood to die at the moment. It was painful. I was pain avoidant. I also didn't want to ruin my clothes.

"Cal? Resilient? He bawled like a baby when he got blood on his sweater," Baz said, and he wasn't wrong, though I would have preferred that we never talk about that incident again. Er, *those* incidents. "No, sorry, Ferris. Cal is properly immortal. Compared to him, the Fae are weaklings. When he goes all Reap—"

I made a sound in the back of my throat that was more threat than cough. Baz immediately shut up, mouthing an apology in my direction. None of these people knew I was a Reaper, and I wanted to keep it that way. I'd not had occasion to use my Reaper abilities since my soul was returned to me, but I knew that it would be dangerous to just about everyone around me. No, for now, I was content to be just Cal. Death's marketing agent and Life's Guy Friday.

"The fact is," I said, trying to take control of the conversation again, "that the Fae are involved in this curse. They can be brought down by capturing and killing them, which is difficult, or outsmarting them."

"And how do we do that?" Richard asked. "Challenge them to a duel? A battle of wits? Riddles or chess or something?"

Baz winced. I couldn't blame him. That was a terrible idea.

"We have to find whoever made a deal with them," I said. "Fast."

"Why such a hurry?" Valerie asked. She held up a hand when the entire band, excepting her grandson, gave her an incredulous look. "Yes, I know that you're having a difficult time with the festival, given that your instruments are being rearranged and such, but surely that's not so bad."

"Things are getting worse," Baz said. Ferris frowned at this, looking at my forehead, where I had a butterfly bandage over the cut from falling off the stage. "And now that they have Cal's blood…"

"That's bad," I said. "Very bad."

"I thought you were a big, dangerous monster," Ferris said, though I could tell she was taking this marginally more seriously than she had done. Maybe it was the cut on my head, or maybe the bat we'd captured, or something else entirely. No, I gathered sarcasm was her method of coping when there was no paperwork to be found, and I couldn't blame her. It was, after all, highly effective.

"That's the point." How to explain this without giving everyone nightmares? "Blood magic is…well, let's just say that those who use it are hunted down. It's a perversion, forcing someone to do your bidding. With such a small sample, I doubt they'd be able to do more than just nudge me in a certain direction, but even that much could cause damage."

"A large part of my job is hunting down those who use blood magic," Baz said, which was news to me. Granted, he and I never really talked about the finer details of our jobs, sharing only the weird or funny stories. We both knew full well how dangerous and cruel the world was, and given that he was the embodiment of Justice, and I was, well, me, sharing the darker details didn't seem kind. But in the way that my cousin swallowed, his mouth a thin line, I could tell that he'd seen and done things in the last months that had changed him.

Some of the carefree nature that had so annoyed me was gone.

I mourned that loss far more than I had expected.

"Whoever is doing this is likely way out of their depths. This may have started with just trying to give the other bands grief, spring-boarding them to the forefront of the festival, but it's going to get worse. Much worse." Baz shook his head, and suddenly I was glad for the sunglasses that hid his eyes.

"What do we do?" Jacques asked, looking at his grandmother, worried.

"Don't you fret," she said, beaming at him. "I can take care of myself. Don't you forget whose recipe book—"

"Yes, yes, you have a recipe for summoning Death," Jacques said on a groan. "I know. You're badass, I shouldn't worry."

"Language!" Valerie sniffed. "Even if it true."

"Cal," Ferris interrupted, looking uncomfortable with the family bonding. "Should we really get these people involved?"

"They're already involved," I pointed out, to which

the band and Valerie nodded eagerly. "We may as well get their help."

Ferris took in a breath through her nose, then she shook her head. "Fine. It's dangerous, though, getting civilians involved. But I can't go about explaining curses and agents of Death and Fae to my colleagues in a request for backup." Her eyes flicked to the cut on my head again, then to the ancient carpet.

"Nothing we can do about that now!" Valerie said cheerfully. She clapped her hands. "Now, what can I do to help?"

"You know magic," I said. "Can you put protection spells around the various stages? Steve, I don't know if you can help with that—"

"I can help," Steve muttered. He gave what I hoped was meant to be a smile to Valerie, one half of his face twisted into a strange grimace, the other caught somewhere between shock and horror. Thankfully, Valerie didn't seem fazed, just smiling benevolently at the young punk witch rocker. Punk rocker witch? I'd have to figure out the terminology later.

"Good. If you can put protection spells around the stages, that should give the bands a bit of a safety net, though Faerie magic is persistent. And if a Fae is involved directly, then those spells won't do much," I said. "Still, it's a start."

"And what about you?" the kindly grandmother asked, looking concerned. "How are you going to hunt down whoever is doing this?"

"Baz, Agent Ferris, and I will be wandering around the festival, looking for anything, ah, out of the ordinary. Mostly, though, I will be…" I sighed, wondering if there were possibly a better way to flush out a jealous musician who would go to such lengths as making a deal with the Fae. Probably, I just couldn't think of one right now. "I will be offering marketing packages to the bands to see if I can figure out which one is desperate to get all the others out of the way."

Silence met my proposal.

Then, from Alice, "Marketing?" She snickered into her hand. "No offense, Cal, but you work for Death, what do you know about marketing?"

I pinched the bridge of my nose. "I'm actually Death's marketing agent," I mumbled, so quietly I hope that no one heard.

Silence again.

I opened one eye, saw everyone except for Baz gaping at me, and promptly closed my eye again. Finally, Agent Ferris started laughing. Deep belly laughs, the sort that were impossible to fake.

"You! A marketing agent for Death!" She was guffawing, now, and I was beginning to feel a bit offended.

"Yes, I'll have you know. I'm the best marketing agent in Elsewhere!" I pulled out my phone, opened the various social media apps for the residents of Elsewhere, and shoved it at the incredulous FBI agent. She fell silent, scrolling through the phone, her expression becoming increasingly shocked.

"Wow," she said. "This is impressive."

"Let me see," Alice said, but Ferris kept my phone just out of reach.

"I didn't know you could sell coffee in quite so many ways. And is that a nymph dance troupe? Wow. What's this? I didn't know you did karaoke, Cal."

I yelped and snatched my phone back, quickly closing it before anyone could try and take it away from me. Baz was laughing and making no secret of it. The karaoke in question was from my recent adventure to get my soul back. I'd had to do karaoke to get information, and the result was exceptionally bad. So bad, in fact, that the proprietor of the bar had sworn that the recording would never see the light of day. Unfortunately, such things rarely proved to be true, and it was now all over Elsewhere.

Apparently, judging by the comments, I gave nightmares to children.

I couldn't tell if I was a laughingstock or even more terrifying to the denizens of Elsewhere. Yolanda and Agravane assured me that I was terrifying, but I didn't believe them. Not when they tried not to smile while telling me that.

"Anyways, yes, I'm a marketing agent. Ask Baz if you don't believe me," I said. "I used to work at Harcourt Marketing before being hired by Death, and they're quite well known, so I should be able to trade on that name if nothing else."

"Harcourt Marketing?" Richard asked, narrowing his eyes. "Bertie, didn't we try to secure a deal with them a while back?"

"Yeah! We were refused, couldn't even get past the assistant to have a conversation with the so-called marketing expert." Bertie shook his head. "Would have been great for our European sales, too."

I coughed. It was possible, probable even, that I'd been the one to refuse the band's proposal. If the time-line was correct, then I was the one who often dealt with people and products to do with the arts. Perhaps I wouldn't mention that to them. Ever.

"So you're some big shot marketing agent," Alice said, folding her arms. Was it just me, or did she sound disappointed that I was Death's marketing agent? "What's that going to do against this Faerie?"

"It's not the Fae we're trying to lure out," Baz said. I nodded.

"We need to find whoever summoned them. Whoever is making a deal with them to perpetrate this curse. If we can find them, then our chances of making this all go away before someone gets hurt go way, way up. Chances are they're a musician."

Ferris nodded. "I can see that. Musician cursing the competition so that they get a better chance at the spotlight. A curse isn't the most conventional method, but I've seen similar things happen before."

Alice huffed, tossing her head. "Fine. So you're going to, what, host some sort of marketing extrava-ganza to draw them out?"

"Basically."

"I still think we should just shut down the festival," Ferris muttered. When Baz started to protest, she held up her hands. "I know, I know, it's better to catch this person than let them wander around causing more problems. We'll do the marketing scheme."

"And why didn't you mention this marketing skill of yours when we first summoned you, hmm?" The singer leaned forwards, fixing me with a direct, slightly terrifying stare. Unfortunately for her, I was reasonable immune to all stares from people not threatening me bodily harm.

"Because I do marketing for Death," I said. "Not human musicians. Also, I don't actually like your music."

"Cal," Baz sighed. "Really?"

"What? It's true!"

The band bristled at me, all except Jacques, who had his eyes raised to the ceiling and looked like he was trying to keep from saying something very rude. I scowled at one of the more intricate blood stains on the wall.

Just then, the bat gave a shriek and rattled the case it was being kept in. Everyone jumped, Ferris even going so far as to draw her gun on the thing. She flushed from chin to hairline a moment later and put her gun away.

"Don't worry, everyone. My cousin may have terrible taste in music, but he is very, very good at his job. We'll get this sorted out in a trice!" Baz clapped and smiled. "Now, how about we run over the plan again?"

CHAPTER 6

"So, what, are you with some sort of record company?" This was the third skeptical singer I'd spoken with in the course of an hour. She was very tall, curvy, and wore a dress so covered in glitter that I couldn't bring myself to meet her gaze, as I was distracted by the sparkles. Honestly, I couldn't even tell you what colour her hair was, given that I couldn't stop staring at the glitter.

"No, I'm a marketing agent," I said. "Harcourt Marketing."

"Never heard of them." The singer crossed her arms, making her dress shine brighter. "Why would you be going around offering marketing packages to the bands? Desperate for work, are you? I don't want some sort of subpar publicity; do you have any idea how much work I've put into my social media presence. I had to hire a video editor for my YouTube channel! I won't waste time on some wannabe who—"

"Whoa, let's be civil here," Baz cut in, smiling his

charming smile. The singer's dress reflected off his sunglasses, which was probably good, because otherwise I had the irrational urge to punch my cousin in the face. Instead, I tried to focus on glitter. "Cal is actually highly renowned for his marketing. That sports medicine guy who scaled that mountain? Yeah, Cal did the work for him."

The singer appraised me with slightly less hostility. "You did that?"

"Among other things," I said. "Currently, I'm trying to learn more about the music industry, and so am expanding my repertoire. I thought it would be good to give a leg up to a lesser known band rather than one who is already established. Practising my skills and such."

Thankfully, she bought it. "So, what, you're offering a free marketing package to a band at the festival? Like a competition?"

It was the only way I could think to draw out whoever was cursing the other musicians. Adding a competition to the festival, instead of the local exposure that was all that was currently on offer, would draw attention. To me, as well as the bands. Yes, it had the possibility of making things worse, but as I'd explained to Agent Ferris during her third protest about the risk, I would also be caught up in the crosshairs and could maybe do something about it.

Frankly, I was making this up as I went, and desperately hoping that Tiny Dinosaurs with Phasers didn't win the contest. Given that I'd already insulted their music, I didn't think I could survive the humiliation of them winning the contest.

"It'll be social media based," I said. "Done through the music festival page. Visitors get to vote on who they liked best, and who they thought had the best showmanship, flair, costumes, the like. So it's not just about how many fans you have, but the quality of the show."

It was mostly about how many fans they had.

The singer shifted her weight again, making the spangly dress shine. It really was hypnotic, so much so that I nearly missed her words. "Alright, fine. But if there's any more of this weird crap, then I'm pulling out entirely, marketing package or no."

I must have hesitated a bit too long, distracted as I was, because Baz nudged me, still with his winning smile pasted over his features. "What sort of weird crap? We've only just arrived, but people seem to be talking about some strange goings on. More than the usual music festival shenanigans, I mean."

"Yeah, we heard something about a bat earlier," Baz said, nodding eagerly. The singer shifted her weight, scratching her arm. She looked about, as if checking to see if anyone was listening, then leaned in.

"I don't know about any bats, but I heard that two bands had to drop out of the festival entirely due to food poisoning. Well, food poisoning, and covid, and a broken foot—the drummer, you see—and a back injury, and sunburn from the stage lights. Who gets sunburned from stage lights?!" The singer shivered, and I was inclined to join her. That sounded distinctly unpleasant. "Not only that. I've had two costumes destroyed by food being spilled all over them, while they were hanging up. In the trailer attached to my car. Where there is no food."

I winced in sympathy. "And this stuff is happening to everyone?"

"Most everyone. Everyone I've talked with, at least. The festival opens tomorrow. A bunch of bands aren't sure it's a good idea to continue, but we all really want to play."

I hoped that an influx of innocent bystanders in the form of an audience would make whoever was doing this back off a bit. If I was right that the Fae were involved, though, backing off wouldn't necessarily be an option. They were manipulative, cold creatures who delighted in people getting the wrong end of a deal while they won out.

"Well, thanks," I said, holding out my hand to shake. "I appreciate you taking the time to talk with us. Just send me your info via my email and we'll be sure to add you to the competition."

"No problem," the woman said, already fishing out her phone to start compiling information to send my way. "See you around, I guess."

Baz and I went on our way, seeking out the next band on the register given to us by Ferris. We'd spoken with about half of the performers, and each one of us had told stories about things that were going on. Some overlapped, but mostly they were all different. Which meant that this curse was big and chaotic. I hated big and chaotic.

"What do you think?" Baz asked after we had gone through just about every band on the list. "Any of them look like viable suspects?"

"Not really." It was annoying. "They've all been impacted by this curse, and frankly none of them seem all that competitive. Most of them aren't even all that interested in my marketing package, say they're doing just fine on their own."

A bit of a blow to the ego, but what could I do? Shove marketing down their throats? No thank you. I just bought this blazer.

Baz wrinkled his nose and shrugged. "There has to be an easy way to draw out whoever's doing this. Could you find the Fae, maybe?"

I shook my head. "Those Faeries that live in the mortal realms have a diminished power, due to there being less magic here. Whoever is doing this likely came through a portal or the veil from Elsewhere. This is beyond what any of the local Fae could do, so far as I know. Granted, most of my knowledge of the locals is tied up in the mob, so maybe I'm the wrong person to ask. Either way, finding an individual Fae in Chicago? Even one summoned from Elsewhere? It'd be impossible. If they were standing ten feet in front of me, maybe."

"Too bad your girlfriend's not here. She's good at hunting people down." Baz grinned at me. I tried not to deflate, his words hitting me like a blow. I sniffled, and my cousin immediately frowned. "Oh, man. What did I do this time? It's not that you're not capable, Cal, but—

"

"I miss Neja!" I wailed, nearly at the point of falling to my knees and throwing a proper tantrum. Baz awkwardly patted my back until I managed to get myself under control.

"Still having some instability issues, I take it?" he asked.

I nodded.

"Well, how about we finish up with this list and we'll go find a nice hotel, call it a night. I bet there are some nice restaurants here and—"

"You're the marketing guys, right?" The speaker was young, maybe eighteen, with the good looks of the genetically blessed, an expression of eagerness on his face. He had dark hair swept back, bright blue eyes, a smile that should have been in movies, and a physique that took a great deal of work. His youth, coupled with that bright-eyed innocence, told me that he either was an exceptional musician to have made it to the festival, or he was way out of his depth.

I exchanged a glance with my cousin. He casually adjusted his sunglasses.

"I'm Cal Thorpe," I said. "The marketing guy, as you so put it. This is Baz."

Baz grinned his most charming grin and waved. "Hi. You with a band?"

The kid shrugged. "I'm, ah, on my own. I sing and play guitar. Grant Keeling."

Keeling. An unfortunate name for anyone trying to make it big. Too many alliterative words. Still, he wasn't on my list of festival musicians, so I was intrigued. "I don't recognise the name. Did you register late?"

The kid blushed bright pink, shuffling a shoe on the pavement. "Well, I sort of, um...I'm a roadie for the festival. Working on stage two, mostly. I thought maybe one of the bands might give me a shot at auditioning, but they're all so busy with everything, and there really isn't time before the festival starts, and..." Grant trailed off. He smiled weakly. "I heard you were offering a marketing package, and I thought that maybe I could play a song for you? Show you what I can do?"

"Listen, Grant, I'm not a manager, or an agent. I only do marketing," I said, holding up my hands.

"That's okay! These days it doesn't really make sense in the music industry to have an agent or a manager because the record companies are just as bound by algorithms and social media as everyone else. Going indie is almost better, because you get to keep all your royalties. You have to market yourself, though, to stand out from the crowd. But marketing is hard. And expensive." He shrugged and winced. Definitely over eager. "Anyways, I thought I'd ask."

I glanced at Baz, who scratched his nose and pushed his sunglasses up higher. Of course my cousin would be so very much help in this. I don't know why I bothered most of the time.

"Well, we were just about to head out for the day. Get a hotel, some food. I have to sort some stuff out, given all the weirdness that's been going on." I kept my expression as neutral as I could, wondering just how eager—or desperate—this kid was.

"Yeah, weird stuff," Grant said. He shoved his hands into his pockets. "I heard someone, uh, fell into a speaker and cracked a toe."

I'd heard a great deal worse about the woman who fell into the speaker. It had been plugged in, after all. Luckily, they were only mild electrical burns. "Exactly. Weird stuff. Listen, Grant, why don't you send me an email, maybe with some links to your videos or website. I'll look it over, and if I like your stuff, we can talk tomorrow."

I handed over a slip of paper with my email on it; Grant snatched it out of my fingers like it was gold. He beamed at me and Baz, clutching the paper in his hand. "Absolutely! Thank you, Mr. Thorpe. You won't be disappointed."

With that, he gave a sort of bob of his head, spun on his heel, and fled, a joyful lilt to his steps.

Baz and I watched him go, waiting until he disappeared behind one of the stages. Baz let out a low whistle. "That's him, do you think?"

"Young, attractive, desperate? Yep. That's him."

"Come on, Cal, he's just a kid. How much damage do you think he could do?" Baz shook his head. "Don't you remember how eager we were at that age?"

I'd been busy with my degree at that point. Baz had been bouncing around from job to job, girlfriend to girlfriend. "I remember exactly how much trouble you got the both of us into at that age. Besides, there's eagerness, and then there's desperation. Either way,

Grant Keeling has fallen in way over his head. He made a deal with the Fae, Baz. The Fae. And in doing so, he's cursed an entire music festival, resulting in property damage, injuries, and a whole slew of accidents that are just plain weird."

"Yeah, that story about the curry..." Baz shivered.

"Indeed." I watched the spot where Grant had disappeared. Then I reached up and touched my head, where the bandage covered the injury I'd gotten earlier. "He's doing a lot of damage. And if we don't rein in this curse, he could be the direct cause of a whole lot more than just minor damage."

"So how do we stop him?"

"I'm working on it. Now, let's go find some food. I'm starving. Oh, and a hotel. I'm *not* staying at that place where your Tiny Dinosaurs are. I have my limits."

"Yeah, yeah, we'll get you a luxury hotel with room service." Behind his glasses, I would have bet that Baz was rolling his eyes. "Come on, Cal, let's go find Special Agent Ferris and Valerie. Maybe invite them to dinner. They might have some ideas about the kid."

A dinner with an FBI agent and an occult grandmother? Wonderful.

CHAPTER 7

We did, in fact, find a hotel with room service. One nice enough to have a separate sitting area from the bedroom, where Baz, Valerie, Ferris and I gathered over our meal. Ferris had a stack of papers, Valerie had her picnic basket, and I had my phone opened to Grant Keeling's social media. For a kid who had grown up with technology and social media, his online presence was woefully prepared, more of a smattering of videos that were poorly edited than anything. No posts engaging with people, no personal information to create a connection, not even a website.

For someone wanting to be a musician, he didn't know much about promoting his music. Not that marketing was easy for the amateur, and there were a lot of amateurs out there to act as competition. I'd watched one of the videos, though, and apart from poor sound quality and bad editing, he was actually reasonably talented.

Too bad he'd chosen to get involved with the Fae rather than seek out promotional help.

"Well, you were right, Cal," Valerie said, stabbing her pasta with surprising vigour. "We took that bat to the park at dusk, and as soon as we started walking about, it tried to fly back through the veil. Let it go and that was that! Easy as pie. Poor thing was just lost, I'm sure. A music festival is no place for a bat."

"I've been doing some research," Ferris cut in, flipping through her papers. "Grant Keeling was hired on as a roadie a month ago. He apparently applied to be in the festival some six months back, but was rejected almost pro forma. Didn't even make the first round of cuts. Him and about six thousand other people, that is."

Valerie clicked her tongue, though I wasn't sure if it was because the Special Agent had interrupted her, or out of sympathy for the kid.

"There are better ways to go about getting a career in music. He's young, he could have put in some work learning the social media game," I said. Maybe I was feeling a bit of sympathy for the kid. "It's just not about talent these days. It's about using the internet well. He's good enough that with a bit of effort, in a few years he could have a reasonable following."

"Youth," Valerie sniffed. "Always impatient. My Jacques for example. Good job with the symphony, but it wasn't exciting enough. Wasn't fast paced enough. So he quits and joins a punk band!"

Baz mumbled something around a mouthful of food that sounded suspiciously like "good music." I pretended to not hear so we wouldn't get into a debate on the merits of Tiny Dinosaurs with Phasers. It wouldn't end well for either of us. I know because we'd had the debate before, and I accidentally ended up spreading the music across Elsewhere. One little internet poll asking for people's opinions and suddenly I've created a music sensation.

No, I was *not* getting into that argument again.

"Unfortunately for Grant, he's going to be paying for the impetuousness of youth," I said. "We have to get him to break the bargain with the Fae. Or the curse will get worse."

"Steve and I put countercurses on all the stages," Valerie said. She patted her picnic basket fondly. "It's only chalk underneath the stages—and let me tell you, these old bones do not fit underneath stages anymore —but it should do well enough for minor injuries and property damage."

"Things seem to have escalated past minor injuries and property damage," Ferris muttered. "Electrical burns? Food poisoning so bad it nearly killed people? This thing is getting worse. We need to stop it. Now. Before the festival opens tomorrow."

I shook my head. "I can't. I have to confront Grant, and get him to break with the Fae, which is highly dangerous in of itself. If he doesn't do it right, or if I can't convince him to do it at all, then the Fae bargain is going to spin out of control. If you cancel the music festival, things will only get worse; the backfire would be fatal for Grant, and probably whoever is in his immediate vicinity."

"Poor kid." Valerie clucked her tongue again.

"That poor kid has put lives at risk," Baz said, his tone surprisingly dark. "He has tried to take things that he hasn't earned, at the expense of other people. He may be young, but he isn't innocent. Don't forget that."

Sometimes *I* forgot that my cousin was now the embodiment of Justice. The carefree Baz I grew up with was still there, but he was more serious, now. Bound to a cause. He'd always been outspoken about his views, a bit too fond of defending right from wrong, even when he was on the outside of the law, but it felt different, now. Deeper.

"So what exactly are you going to do?" Ferris asked, leaning back. She crossed her arms and all but glared at me. "Just let this thing play out?"

"The contest will run itself now that I've spread the word, and will likely draw the attention of the Fae who put the curse on things. We just need to be there to watch. Get Grant and the Fae in the same place at the same time. Keep all the other musicians safe. We just need to be on hand to contain any magical attacks, as much as possible."

"With what?" Valerie looked at her picnic basket. "I've only enough for simple countercurses, and we've placed them at the stage. Doing more active magic is beyond me. I'm not that kind of witch, dear. And poor Steve isn't either. You need something a bit more powerful."

Ferris let out a long breath, still watching me. "Couldn't you do what you did before?"

"What *exactly* did I do before?" I'd been in too many

unfortunate situations and drawn a whole lot of attention to know what she was talking about.

"Take on the spell? You were the target of that death magic or whatever it was, back with Dermot Green. Pretty sure it was meant for him, or do you honestly expect me to believe that someone aimed to kill a tax collector over a mafioso?"

I winced. "Okay, first of all, nobody likes tax collectors. But, yes, I did take on the death wish meant for Green. That was an accident, though. The wisher pointed at the wrong person. I don't know how to replicate it, let alone with a curse like this. I work for Death, not Sorcerers Incorporated."

Baz snorted.

"They have your blood, though, don't they?"

Ferris may have had a point. A tiny one.

"The fact that they have my blood could be very useful—it takes a whole lot to do me any real harm and I will draw their attention—or it could be very bad." My voice was low. "Very, very bad."

Valerie waved a dismissive hand. "Pah! You're a bit skinny to be much of a threat. And I doubt you could hold a weapon, let alone hurt anyone with it."

That may not have been strictly true. My soul, during his sojourn outside my body, had picked up quite a bit of combat training in order to fend off the big bad monsters who liked to snack on energy. It was possible that I picked up those skills when my soul returned. I had only tested the theory once, and that was under circumstances of great stress, so I wasn't sure how capable I actually was. No, my ability to fight wasn't the problem. The problem was that I was a Reaper. A being that gave most people nightmares at the very least and waking terrors more often than not. And I had Death's heart beating beside my own. I had gone toe to toe with powerful beings, and I'd won.

If someone could use blood magic on me, then we could all be in a lot more danger than anyone realised.

"I don't even know if blood magic works on me," I said, more to buy time than anything. The truth was, I had no idea what I was doing. Magic like this was out of my depth. I didn't know how to stop it.

"Couldn't we make a bargain with the Fae? Counteract Grant's agreement?"

Baz and I both winced at Ferris' question. My cousin, thankfully, answered with a great deal more tact than I would have done. "That becomes very complicated. Fae are bound to honour their agreements, so they won't make counteracting offers or risk being torn apart. It's…well, it's like asking a lawyer to defend and prosecute at the same time. It doesn't work."

"That's it?" Ferris asked, scowling. "That's all the advice you can offer? Don't make a deal with the Fae?"

"Sorry," Baz said on a shrug.

"This sort of magic is not something I've really done before." I prodded my food with my fork, appetite diminished.

Ferris scoffed, but said nothing further. Valerie, too, fell into silence and since I was trying not to draw attention to my particular brand of dangerous, focused entirely on eating my food.

"Well, we can try our best tomorrow," Valerie said at last. "I'll see if I can't make some charms tonight, for the bands, maybe counteract some of the bad magic. It might do more than the countercurse will by itself."

I nodded my thanks. Ferris swiped her papers and stalked from the room, grumbling about useless civilians. I was left with Baz, who studied his plate.

"You have no idea what you're doing, do you?" he said at last.

"Not a clue."

"Well then. You'd better get a good night's sleep before we walk into absolute chaos tomorrow."

With that, my cousin left for his own room. I took his advice, texting Neja an update of my situation before going to bed. I'd hoped that my girlfriend would respond, but she was likely busy with her own work. I slipped into sleep with uncertainty digging into my spine.

For the duration of my soul being missing, I hadn't dreamed. When I regained my soul, my dreams were strange, like memories that I couldn't quite see, but they always left me unsettled and slightly paranoid. Death had said that the paranoia was normal, a reaction to being whole again when I'd been used to being in pieces for so long. Yolanda had just upgraded security around the office to make me feel better. Agravane did his best to scare me by hiding around corners. He got coffee thrown on him more than once.

This dream was different.

For one, I was standing on stage at the music festival, crowds of faceless people walking by. Music—

intangible, strange, even discordant—filtered through the air, not quite loud enough to hear properly, but not quiet enough to ignore. There was no one else on stage with me, only a few instruments that had been discarded. None of them looked like they belonged to this century, let alone at a music festival. A harp, gilded and adorned with a dragon's head. A dulcimer. A lute. A harpsichord.

"Don't you just love the taste of mortal admiration?"

I turned to face the newcomer, a tall, aristocratic male that was too perfect to be human. He was predominantly gold, with burnished skin, yellow-gold hair, and clothes that were gilded in various shades of the colour. He had high cheeks, straight nose, and a mouth that was sensual and just the tiniest bit cruel. His eyes were a violet that looked more floral than anything, like they'd been picked from a garden. He was designed to entrance, to gather attention, to trick humans and other lesser magical creatures into doing his bidding. A Faerie, then. From the Summer court, perhaps. Spring, even.

"I can't say that it matters much to me," I replied evenly, turning away from the Fae and looking back into the crowd. The faceless people were turning one by one to stare at the Fae, and I could practically feel their interest as something tangible on the skin.

"Oh, come now, Lost Reaper, surely admiration means *something* to you." The Fae smiled, an entrancing movement that was strangely graceful. "After all, who doesn't like to be admired every now and again?"

"Trust me, if you'd heard me sing you would never

offer me admiration. I prefer a nice, quiet existence, doing my work. Alas, Life seems to have other plans, but I do what I can." I shrugged.

The Fae hummed, giving me a coy smile. He started wandering around the stage, going up to each instrument and caressing them, though he didn't play. "Do you not just love music?" he asked. "And human music, too! Oh, how grand it is. So inventive. A shame that we Fae were not blessed with such creativity. We can only create the imitation of art, not the thing itself. But humans! They can create *wonders*."

"Is that why you attached yourself to Grant Keeling?" I asked, because who else would be invading my dreams at this moment. "Because you like his music?"

"The boy has the talent to take on the world, yes," the Fae mused, fingers running delicately over the strings of the lyre. "But I fear he lacks the will to see the thing through. Foolish boy, he doesn't understand that those on the top stand upon those below."

"Your methods are making him uncomfortable?" This was good news for me; it meant that I could maybe convince Grant to break the deal with the Fae.

The creature shrugged one shoulder, looking at me with interest. "Now *you* are a being of much power. Yet those upon which you stand all had blood on their hands. The Reapers are all like that, I suppose. Sanctimonious, refusing to do harm unless their victim made a choice. That's the problem with you Movers Between. Always firm in your boundaries. But *you*, you aren't like the other Reapers."

The Fae drifted closer, nostrils flaring like he was

taking my scent. I remained perfectly still, wondering just what he knew about the other Reapers. They'd been gone for a century, at least, likely longer. No one seemed to know what happened to them, only that they vanished. Even Death had grown quiet when I asked, and Life changed the subject. I was, so far as I knew, the last Reaper. And yet this Fae talked like the others were still around. Was that some trick of an immortal's sense of time? Or was it more?

"You smell of humanity," he said, dancing a finger across my shoulder. "Humanity and the edges of existence. Melded together in the body of a Reaper. Tell me, how is that possible?"

My two hearts beat loudly in my ears, not quite in sync. My vision became grey, colour leeching out of the world as the Reaper part of me rose to the forefront. I blinked it back, not wanting to provoke the Fae, and not wanting him to see that he'd provoked me.

"What would it take for you to end the curse on the festival?" I asked, moving the conversation to a more comfortable subject. "To set Grant Keeling free of his bargain?"

"A great deal more than you can afford." The Fae grinned, taking two steps back from me. He took in a deep breath, arms spread wide, and the faceless people in the audience started screaming, just as fans at a rock concert would do. "The taste of admiration is so sweet. Besides, one should not turn one's back on family."

I hissed. Grant was family to this creature. He was half-fae at least, a changeling at most. That made breaking the curse all the more complicated, since it was likely fuelled by Grant just as much as this Fae.

"What about my blood? What would it cost to get that back?" I asked. Maybe if I made a small bargain, I could twist it against the Fae, incapacitate him. But the infuriating creature just smiled wider, showing off pointed teeth.

Eyes glinting he said, "Neither me nor mine have your blood, Reaper. But what I would give to have a sample of that myself."

In a crash of music and a flash of light, the Fae vanished and I woke up.

The Fae didn't have my blood. Which meant there was someone else involved. Bother.

CHAPTER 8

I relayed what information I'd learned to Baz the next morning on our way to the music festival. To my surprise, he let out a string of curses, startling the poor barista making our coffee. I apologised in my best posh accent, which earned me a confused smile, then hurried my cousin from the coffee shop.

"You've made a few enemies, Cal," Baz grumbled. "Any number of them could be behind this."

"Oh, come on, I haven't made *that* many enemies," I complained.

"Both the Summer and Winter courts of Fae? The dreaming giants? The exousia? A fair few of the rock trolls? What about Fate? Or—"

"I get the point," I grumbled, taking a sip of my coffee. I winced; this drink was insipid and bitter at the same time, definitely not up to snuff. With a disappointed sigh, I debated tossing it. Coffee was coffee, though, and I needed my morning hit of caffeine before dealing with the irascible Special Agent Ferris and the cheery Valerie. Not to mention the overeager punk band and half-Fae musician hoping for glory. Oh, and a Faerie had invaded my dreams last night, which had me in even more of a mood.

"Not to mention that you're a powerful enough entity in Elsewhere to draw attention of people you haven't offended personally," Baz continued, completely ignoring my glare as he waved his scone about. "I imagine there are sorcerers who would pay a handsome bounty for a bit of your blood, as the Fae suggested. Or someone looking to hold one over on you for future use. You know as well as I that Elsewhere is dangerous and full of blackmail."

Oh, yes, that made me feel a whole lot better. "I don't know much about blood magic, but I'm fairly certain the sample has to be used quickly, before it dries up or whatever. And they didn't get a lot, which means some of the bigger spells are out of the picture."

Baz shook his head, completely ignoring me. "We need to figure out who else is involved, and quickly, before things get bad."

"I just thought I'd wait and see. Maybe do some sightseeing. Window shopping. I hear there are some reasonable bookstores in town," I deadpanned.

Baz rounded on me, alarm showing even through his sunglasses. "Are you even taking this seriously?!"

"Of course I am. Do you honestly think I don't know how dangerous all this is? How problematic it is to have someone running around with a sample of *my* blood. I don't mean to be arrogant, but I'm not something to mess around with, and if someone is going to try using blood magic on me, then we have a serious calamity on our hands. The only thing is, Baz, I have no idea how to find this person. As you so kindly pointed out, I have a number of enemies, and there are always people who would be happy to get a scrap of my hide to further their own cause. It could be anyone." I took another sip of the terrible coffee and snarled in disgust, throwing the cup into the nearest rubbish bin. A woman in a business suit walking past eyed me with wariness, then hurried on. Baz watched her go, the fight drained out of him.

"We can ask Valerie," he suggested quietly. "She seems to know more than most humans."

I snorted. "We'd be better off asking my mother. Valerie knows a few spells, and certainly she's *aware* of the arcane, but do you honestly think she would have any idea of who would want to steal the blood of a Reaper? She thinks I'm Death's marketing agent, for goodness sakes."

"And you are," Baz assured me. I hunched my shoulders.

"Ostensibly, perhaps. But I have been a great deal more than that for some time. From the beginning, perhaps, as much as I would like to deny it." I shook my head and kept walking. As we drew nearer the music festival, I began to hear noises of bands warming up, as well as see signs of interest from passersby. "For now, let's just focus on the curse, okay? Grant Keeling is probably half-fae, if not a changeling. That means he's going to be tied up in this magic more concretely.

Undoing the bargain isn't going to be as simple as him changing his mind. We'll have to actually break it externally."

"How?" Baz asked, playing along with me for now. "We don't even know what the terms of the bargain are."

I winced. He was right. "And I doubt he or his father are going to tell us. So we have to guess."

"The bands have been targeted exclusively, not the technicians or the roadies. So that means that Grant is trying to get them out of the festival. To, what, open up space for him to play? The producers of the festival already rejected his suit once."

I shrugged. "Maybe if they're desperate enough, they would let him play."

"So we don't let him play," Baz said. "We keep the other bands in the festival, and we don't let him play, even as a side line show or busker."

The festival was three days long. Stopping one musician from playing a single note during that time would be extremely difficult. Still, I had Ferris and Valerie and the Tiny Dinosaurs at my disposal. Surely we could sort it out one way or another.

Baz and I made it to the festival just as the gates were opening. The early morning attendees were mostly young people, either college age or just starting out in business. Those who thought that spending a whole day at a music festival would be fun rather than exhausting. I envied their energy. I imagined that more people would trickle in throughout the day, coming to see certain bands or just stay for the afternoons or evenings. Either way, it would be busy.

Agent Ferris met us at the gate, waving us through security with little issue, especially as I wasn't sporting bunny slippers anymore. Valerie was already waiting for us, wearing the brightest yellow sundress I've ever seen, with a massive straw hat covered in bits and bobs. I peered closer and had to adjust my glasses several times to be sure I was seeing things right.

"Are those peace signs? Made out of sticks?"

"Do you like them? I'm handing them out to every band member at the festival. My good luck charms, if you will." Valerie batted her eyelashes, which was a strange look on a woman of her age. "Steve helped me make them, poor lad. I told him not to worry since he had to be up early for the festival, but apparently he suffers from insomnia. I told him to try chamomile tea, but he just sat up with me and made good luck charms instead."

She handed us two charms, which looked like nothing more than homemade hippie accessories, then went sashaying about on her way, stopping each musician and giving out her charms. No one seemed to stop her, or even get in her way, and everyone took a charm without question, no matter how strange it seemed. I was impressed.

"I wish I could talk to people like that," Ferris said. "You have no idea how much easier interrogations would be."

"No kidding," Baz agreed, sounding wistful.

"Oh, yes, because you need *more* charm." I sniffed,

shaking my head. "Come on, let's go see about keeping all the bands playing."

We filled Ferris in on the general plan on our way to the first stage playing for the day, with the singer in her spangly dress and a backup band of well-dressed individuals. It was fairly straightforward to keep her singing, and the band playing. Valerie and Steve's countercurses seemed to be working well enough, and I made sure to stand around casually mentioning the contest to any fans, making sure that the social media page stayed active and fans engaged.

The rest of the day was more difficult, though. There were, generally, no less than two bands playing at any different time—except for the headliner bands who managed to get a time slot all to themselves—and those first in the morning and about three in the afternoon, when people's attention was considerably lessened. Baz and I split up, Ferris patrolling the grounds as best she could with Valerie.

With only one of us watching for signs of the curse at each stage, it was more difficult to keep track of what was going on. Twice, I thought I saw flares of light from beneath the stage. Signs that the countercurse was working, perhaps, in keeping magic from affecting the bands. When I ducked underneath one stage just before lunch, I could see that the chalk lines were already starting to wear away.

Baz told me via text message that he'd seen at least one drumstick go flying in an improbable direction, and while it didn't stop the band from playing, they were increasingly more wary, given all that had already happened. Ferris reported nothing strange, but she did say that even good bands weren't getting quite as much interest as she would expect, like the audience was continuously distracted. The contest helped, as long as people knew about it, but even with social media contests drawing fans' attention, there was a definite tension in the air.

By four in the afternoon, I was feeling frazzled and exhausted. I'd seen no sign of Grant Keeilng, and I hoped that he was busy doing roadie activities and not planning anything more sinister. There was a brief lull in the musical activity while two bands switched places, and I happily collapsed at a picnic table with the largest cup of iced tea I could purchase for a ridiculous amount of money.

"How are things on your end?" Baz asked, plopping down next to me. He had a bottle of water pressed to his forehead.

"I've seen exactly two lightbulbs burn out on the stage lights, and a guitar pick flew off the stage during a particularly tricky solo, but otherwise everything seems to be alright. Audience isn't very interested in the music, though," I said. Already, the crowds seemed a bit thin for the afternoon rush, most people bent over their phones or in line for overpriced food and drinks.

"I talked with Ferris ten minutes ago, and she says that she hasn't seen anything odd except for a few cables getting tangled. Valerie said that her counter-curses are almost worn out, though, from all the hits they've taken. Thinks that they might last the rest of the day, but not longer than that."

I was surprised we'd gotten that much out of them, to be honest. Then again, I knew next to nothing about witchcraft, so maybe chalk lines were more powerful than I thought.

"What about your favourite band?" I asked. I had studiously avoided the stage where Tiny Dinosaurs with Phasers had played that day, choosing instead to leave that particular honour to Baz and Valerie. I'd had enough of their music in Elsewhere.

Baz winced, rubbing the back of his neck. "Their set did…not go well. Alice and Richard were not in good time, Bertie was too loud, and as far as I could tell, both Steve and Jacques were out of tune."

"Was that part of the curse?" None of the other bands had played badly; their problems seemed to be more in line with general misfortune or clumsiness.

"No." Baz sighed, shoulders slumping. "Alice said they had stayed up all night trying to figure out how to stop the curse, despite none of them but Steve knowing anything about magic. They didn't even do a morning sound check. It was bad."

With any luck, they wouldn't be winning my impromptu contest, then. I wanted absolutely nothing to do with the marketing of Tiny Dinosaurs with Phasers. Still, as I wasn't dumb enough to tell Baz that, I patted him on the shoulder and said nothing.

A few minutes later, Ferris came and sat at our table, looking disgruntled. Her hair was tied up severely, but there were strands escaping her almost militaristic style. Her clothes were professional, but rumpled, and I was fairly certain there was a ticket stub stuck to the bottom of her right shoe. "Never again," she grumbled, stealing Baz's water bottle and cracking the seal. She drank half the bottle in one go.

"That bad?" Baz asked cheerfully, his disappointment over his favourite band's bad performance obviously assuaged by Ferris' discomfort.

"I blame you, Cal," Ferris said, jabbing a finger in my direction. "Ever since the last time you showed up, I've been stuck with the weird cases. The ones that are obviously impossible, or just bizarre. Magical. Supernatural. Whatever. Do you know how many hauntings I've investigated since you came into my life? Twelve. Not one of them was actually viable, yet here I am, stuck with the weird. And it's all your fault."

I shrugged, swirling the straw around in my drink. "I told you not to write up an accurate report. It is your own fault if you're reaping the consequences."

Ferris snarled something quite rude at me. I thought she might even go so far as to throw the half-empty water bottle at my head. Even as she raised the bottle, a crack of thunder filled the air. The sky, which was blue only moments ago, turned stormy and grey, threatening all the festival goers with rain. Thunder and lightning prevailed, drowning out the shrieks of the attendees as they fled for shelter. The magic was so thick in the air that even *I* could feel it.

There was something else there, too.

A song.

I turned towards the music, entranced. It wasn't like anything I'd ever heard before, and I knew that no mere mortal could produce something so lovely. So beautiful. So damning. Before I knew it, I was standing, moving towards the music. It didn't seem anyone else could hear it, because they were all shouting at me, calling me back.

I ignored them.

The music called me through the park, around grass lawns and flower beds, makeshift stages and the permanent amphitheatre around which the festival was centred. I followed it willingly despite someone tugging at my arm. Then, I found it.

A small fountain, bubbling merrily, gleaming coins on the bottom of the basin. Inside, a woman sat, back turned to me, feet resting in the water, hair wet and plastered to her skin. She turned to me, and for a brief moment, I hesitated. Despite the music, she had features that were more predator than woman.

In the back of my mind, I knew what this was. A siren.

She paused in her singing. "Cal Thorpe?" she asked, smiling broadly. "Calvin Montgomery Thorpe?"

"Yes?"

In a flash, the siren had her hand around my wrist. The water in the fountain started churning, frothing. "My master wishes to speak with you."

She pulled me into the water. I tried not to scream.

CHAPTER 9

I don't know if you've ever been on a journey through dimensions. I have. Several times. Generally, it's extremely uncomfortable and leaves a person with an overwhelming sense of vertigo. Sometimes there's joint pain. Not something I would recommend. Travelling through dimensions by means of a siren holding onto your wrist and pulling you through a watery portal?

Well, let's just say that it was a good thing I was incapable of dying.

My lungs filled with water several times over. My vision went white at least once, and when I came around, I was still being dragged behind the siren. Once, she looked back at me, grinning with shark-like teeth. I bit my tongue trying to hold back a scream to conserve air, but my lungs were already on fire and I was fairly certain that my clothes were ruined. Again.

Finally, we emerged from the water. I gasped for breath, dog paddling to the shore a few metres away.

There, I lay on my hands and knees in mud, hacking up water and debris. After a few minutes of this, my lung capacity seemed to recover. I clawed my way farther up the bank and rose to my feet, swaying. My surroundings were blurry, thanks to my wet glasses, but I could make out enough to note that the water I'd emerged from was just a pond. A smallish pond in a pleasantly manicured park. Two ducks paddled around the water, quacking rudely at me. There weren't a lot of people about, but those that were happened to be on the other side with a dog, throwing a ball.

The skyline was what really did me in, though. I, unfortunately, recognised those buildings.

"I'm still in Chicago?!" I spluttered. Rounding on the siren, who floated in the water, smiling wickedly, I threw my arms into the air. "Why in the world did you pull me through a portal if we're still in Chicago?! I could have taken a car, you insensitive maniac!"

The siren laughed.

"Don't blame her."

I spun around, my shoes squelching loudly as I did so. Apparently not all the people in the park were playing with a dog. No, this one looked...well, he sort of looked like me. Except better.

For one, he wasn't soaking wet. But that aside, he had hair two shades darker than mine, artfully tousled. His eyes were brown, but more of a molten brown than my average colour. He had on a suit that was, by all accounts, one of the best you could find in the mortal realms: a charcoal grey wool silk blend, possibly with some cashmere, perfectly tailored, with buttons that were probably actual ebony. His shoes were gleaming leather. His features were also remarkably like my own, though certainly more symmetrical and chiseled. His glasses were designer, black frames, and didn't slide down his nose.

It was a bit like déjà vu, to be honest, me coming face to face with a doppelgänger. Only, this time, I was in full possession of my soul, and my Reaper abilities had integrated fully. As far as I was aware, there were no other bits of me running around on their own. So who was this guy?

"Let me guess," I said, squeezing out my handkerchief and trying to wipe down my glasses. "A clone?"

The man, whoever this better-looking version of me was, snarled. "A *clone*?!"

"Well, I've still got my soul, and last I checked I didn't have any siblings, so—"

Not Actually Me strode forward and grabbed the collar of my shirt, all but lifting me off the ground. "Don't you *dare* mock me."

Geez, he even sounded like me, only better.

"I don't even know who you are! How could I mock you?" I was talented, but even I had my limits.

That was apparently the wrong thing to say. He threw me backwards, enough that I nearly landed in the pond again. The siren let out a wail of delight and swam towards me. I scrabbled back to shore, not really interested in experiencing drowning. Again.

"*You* ruined *my life!*" the man roared.

"How?" I demanded, quite done with the shouting and the manhandling. I'd dealt with enough bullies in my time in Elsewhere to hardly be cowed by this guy, especially since I was pretty sure he was human. "How could I have possibly ruined your life? I don't know you!"

The man spun in a circle, hands to his head. He let out a manic laugh. "Do you know what happened? One day, I went to work, having just received a promotion to vice president of my firm. I was going to move into my new office. I was going to make *plans*. Only, I went into work and people started screaming. Every time they looked at me, they would scream. And when they turned away, it would stop, only to start again when they looked at me. It turns out, they all thought I was dead, but no matter how often I explained that I wasn't, no matter that I was *standing right in front of them*, I couldn't prove that I wasn't dead. Every single person I knew, taken from me overnight."

A sinking feeling settled into my stomach.

The man continued, pacing frantically on the shore. "I could interact with anyone else, though, so long as I didn't use my full name. But any lasting relationships I tried to make, any real permanence, vanished. My leasing agreements suddenly fell through. Banks lost all records of my having ever been a client. It was like I wasn't a part of the world anymore."

My mouth went a bit dry. I coughed.

My better looking look-alike stamped his foot on the ground and jabbed a finger at me. He had a wild gleam in his eye. "Then one day, I witnessed something impossible. A…creature. A wolf, wandering around at dawn, turned into a man. I thought I was finally losing my mind until I began to see things everywhere. Flying people the size of an insect. Cats that could talk. People made of smoke, some with blue skin. Magic. It was magic I was seeing. A whole different world that I'd never noticed before, right before my very eyes. So I started paying attention. And do you know what I heard?"

I had a guess. A very bad guess.

"I heard rumours about a new power wandering around, bound to both Life and Death. A power by the name of Cal Thorpe." The man stepped close enough to jab his finger into my chest. "*My* name."

I winced.

"It took me two *years* to piece everything together. That there was another Calvin Thorpe out there, only with a different middle name, and an 'e' at the end of Thorp. And that *this* Cal Thorpe had been employed by Harcourt Marketing, a direct competitor to my firm, Dubenitch and Green. That *this* Cal Thorpe had died under mysterious circumstances, only to have been hired by Death to be his marketing agent. Do you see where I'm going with this?"

Calvin Thorp glowered at me. I tugged at my very wet sleeves and tried to scrape together some of my dignity. As it turns out, I knew exactly who this was, and why he'd been having such a difficult time of things. See, when Death hired me, apparently there was a mix-up. He was supposed to have hired a Calvin Mason Thorp, marketing extraordinaire, to work for him.

He got me, Calvin Montgomery Thorpe, instead.

Death explained all of this to me after I returned from my soul gathering trip, his heart now embedded in my chest. After I'd learned that Fate—Death's mother—intervened in the hiring so that I would be taken on instead. As Death saw it, things worked out since I was a Reaper, my mother a Knight, and I was actually quite good at marketing.

It would seem, though, that the *other* Cal Thorp hadn't fared so well in the exchange.

He leaned closer, baring his teeth at me in a mockery of a smile. "Well?"

"Ah. Yes. I, ah…It's nice to meet you. I do apologise for any inconvenience. I shall be taking this up with Death immediately, and we can see about getting your life back." I offered up a weak smile of my own, already reaching into my pocket for my phone.

Cal laughed at me and shoved me away. He reached into his jacket pocket and pulled out a handkerchief wrapped around something. Carefully, he unwrapped it, revealing a tiny glass vial with a minuscule amount of liquid in the bottom. Red liquid.

"*My* life ended the day you stole it," Cal sneered. He shook the vial and took a menacing step towards me. "No, I'm going to take *your* life."

Pieces fell into place. He was the one who stole my blood. He was the other player in this game. And if he knew enough sorcery to use blood magic, especially on me, with whom he already had a sympathetic link, then things were going to get very bad. Very, very bad.

Unfortunately for me, when I get into bad situations, I tend to respond in one way: snark.

"How, exactly, do you plan to do that? You've got what, two drops of my blood? Hardly enough for a basic curse, let alone a life switch," I said. Cal hissed through his teeth.

"Do you think I'm an idiot?" he asked. "I've been planning this for *years*. I only needed your blood to draw you here, and now that you're here, I can drain you completely."

"Right. In the middle of a park in Chicago. I'm sure no one will notice or complain." I managed to get to my feet, brushing clumps of mud from my trousers and preparing to run. I wouldn't get far with my wet shoes, but any progress would be better than none.

To my dismay, though, Cal merely smiled. "I've a few more resources than you think, Mr. Thorpe. Elodie, if you would?"

The siren giggled, drawing my attention. Then, she started to sing. This wasn't like before, at the festival, where I'd been aware of the music and its draw on me. This was so much more. Insidious, all-encompassing. The music bored into my mind and the rest of the world slipped away.

My phone fell from my hands and my feet carried me towards the water, even as part of my mind knew that I was moving to my doom. My two hearts beat loudly in my ears, almost enough to drown out the music. My vision went grey, my Reaper abilities rising to do battle with the thing that so entranced me.

Then, the music cut short, stopping with a shriek and a gurgle.

"Stay away from my cousin."

I blinked, vision returning to colour in a rush. Standing with a gun pointed at the siren, who was now underwater and vanishing fast, was Special Agent Ferris. Baz was at her side, sunglasses gleaming darkly. Valerie was beside me, holding out a picnic blanket and looking sympathetic.

"Poor dear! That pond water surely has some terrible bacteria in it. We should get you cleaned up as soon as possible. Get you some soup, too, to warm you up. It's a warm day, but even so. Magical trips through Chicago waterways are sure to weaken the immune system."

I wrapped the picnic blanket around me and muttered my gratitude. Baz approached, frowning at me.

"How did you get here?" I asked. He looked dry, so it likely wasn't by portal.

"Ferris tracked your phone. I installed the app last night." Baz shrugged like it was nothing. Normally, I would have squawked with the invasion of privacy—I had some very embarrassing photos on my phone—but instead I just nodded.

"Did you catch him?" I looked around. Cal was nowhere to be seen.

"Who?" Ferris asked, holstering her gun. "Do you have any idea how I'm going to explain that I discharged my weapon into a pond? I have to fill out paperwork for every bullet fired, and my supervisors are absolutely going to put me on mandatory psych counselling for shooting a pond. It's not like I can say I shot a siren, now is it?"

"Er, thanks," I said. "But we have to catch him."

"Who?" Ferris repeated again.

"Ah." I winced. How to explain this without people screaming at me? "Well, you see, there's this, um, other Cal…"

I explained things as best I could while leaving out any embarrassing descriptions of myself—in no world was I going to tell my cousin that the evil villain was a better-looking version of myself. But by the time I got to the description of my kidnapping and the mistaken employment, Baz was doubled over, arms wrapped around his middle.

Not screaming.

Laughing.

"You got kidnapped by the evil version of you?" Ferris asked.

I sniffed. Adjusted the picnic blanket. "Maybe."

Valerie clucked her tongue again. "There's surely some sort of explanation other than *evil*."

"Oh, I cannot *wait* to tell Yolanda and Agravane and Neja," Baz said, laughing. "And Aunt Teresa! She is going to be so amused."

I winced. My mother would, in all likelihood, be very unamused. Maybe I could bribe Baz into silence.

"Either way, we need to break this curse and capture the other Cal before he figures out a way to put me at the middle of his spell," I said.

"Surely it wouldn't work," Ferris said. "You may have similar stories, but you're, well, you. And he's not."

True. I was a Reaper. I did have Death's heart. I couldn't die. Who knew what this other Cal could do when faced with all of that? Somehow that thought didn't actually make me feel any better about the situation.

"Two forces, almost identical until their paths diverged, coming together again?" Valerie shook her head. "The karmic storm would be devastating."

"How devastating?" Ferris narrowed her eyes.

Valerie frowned. "Well, it would make the curse at the music festival look like a child's trick. What our Mr. Thorpe is wrapped up in would decimate Chicago."

"Again," Ferris said.

"Okay, to be fair, that last one wasn't my fault. I had a death wish attached to me! You can't blame *me* for buildings falling down if I'm the target."

"You'd be surprised," she snarled. "Let's go. We have work to do."

CHAPTER 10

During my abduction, Ferris and Valerie had left the Tiny Dinosaurs in charge of keeping Grant from performing. That meant the music festival was now full of some very confused people wearing a lot of Tiny Dinosaurs with Phasers merchandise. It was extraordinarily comfortable, despite the band's questionable taste in music, which meant they got a large amount of free advertising. Of course, the festival was also a bit extra chaotic, with punk fans screaming their heads off at the slightest burst of music.

"A social media campaign," Bertie explained with pride while I gaped in abject horror at the confusion. "Alice set it up."

I eyed Alice warily as she helped a roadie clear the instruments from the stage for the next band. She beamed at me and waved cheerfully, the effect offset somewhat by the large spiked bracelet around her wrists.

"Any issues while we were gone?" Ferris asked, as

though parades of Tiny Dinosaurs t-shirts wandering around didn't count as an issue. Valerie was already conferring with Steve on the state of the countercurses under the stages.

"Nothing dramatic," Jacques said. "Two fans spilled drinks on stage three while there was a set change. And one of the food trucks had a small fire, but we think that was because they were just really terrible cooks."

I blinked. "Really? Nothing to do with the music or the musicians?"

Richard shrugged. "Not really. I mean, as soon as you left, it got pretty quiet. Quietest it's been all week."

I guess my plan worked. In all the machinations of the social media contest—and the one conversation I'd had with Grant—I must have drawn the attention of the Faerie bargain. It was centred around me, around my watching Grant perform. I was the one who could provide fame and glory, even if indirectly, so I had become the target.

Honestly, with the other Cal Thorp after me as well, being the target of a Faerie bargain felt like one thing too much. I started laughing hysterically.

Baz immediately clamped a hand over my mouth, though that hardly did anything to muffle the sounds coming from my mouth. My cousin smile apologetically. "Sorry about this. Cal is still, ah, a little unstable after getting his soul back. It takes time to readjust, apparently."

That, of course, only made everyone gape at me. Ferris put her hand on her holster, her own version of comfort-seeking. "Got his soul back?" she asked hoarsely.

I laughed harder, dislodging Baz's hands as I doubled over, trying to catch my breath. I was vaguely aware that conversations were being had around me, trying to decide how to stop the hysterics. All I could do, though, was laugh at the irony of the universe. Here I was, a marketing agent, devoting my energy to making other people and products the centre of attention, and yet somehow I'd managed to become the centre of attention myself.

Something hit me over the head. I stumbled forwards, my breath catching in my throat and making me cough. The laughing subsided as I went into a coughing fit, but at least it had stopped.

"That helped?" Baz asked. I looked up to find him staring at Valerie in astonishment. "I could have done that!"

"Then why didn't you?" the old woman asked, smiling sweetly. She patted her picnic basket and turned her grin on me. "So glad you're feeling better! Now I know your ailment, I can make you a nice batch of tea to help balance things out. I'll put something special in it to make it a little stronger. That will help, too."

Before I could refuse that tempting offer, a voice called out to me. "Mr. Thorpe!"

I whirled, hoping that the other Cal hadn't caught up to me. It wasn't him, but I did see Grant Keeling jogging in my direction, holding a guitar case in his hands, an eager look dominating his features. Now that

I knew was he was, I don't know how I had missed it before. He was too attractive to be fully human, and his expressions weren't quite right with just a little too much emotion in them, as if he were trying to seem normal. It was why so many changelings and half-fae were shunned by society; they could never blend in well enough to be accepted and so lived on the outskirts, never quite fitting in. Honestly, I could sympathise with that particular affliction.

I pitied Grant for a moment, then remembered what he was doing to the other musicians here.

"Ah, Mr...." I said, feigning ignorance. I saw the eagerness melt from the kid's face.

"Keeling. Grant Keeling? We spoke yesterday?" he said, fidgeting in place, white-knuckling his guitar case.

"Oh, yes! That's right." Playing the high-and-mighty marketing agent wasn't my favourite task, but one couldn't deny that I was good at it. Really, really good at it. "You've met the band Tiny Dinosaurs with Phasers, haven't you? They're going to be sensational in the near future, I have no doubt."

Grant blinked, a look of astonishment crossing his features before he smiled. It wasn't as wide as before. "Of course! I've helped you guys move some of your gear about. You have the custom fretted bass, don't you?" he asked Steve, who nodded and said nothing, as per usual.

"I hate to dash," I said, looking at my phone, "but I've got a meeting with some design people who have been working on some mockups for the winner of this contest. I want to get everything finalised before the contest is over."

"Oh, uh, sure," Grant said, clutching his guitar case closely. He looked on the verge of devastation. "Can I catch up with you later?"

"Absolutely." Then, without even looking at the desperate changeling, I turned away, head in my phone. Baz jogged up to me, settling in to my stride.

"He's so eager." It was a sad statement, but true. So I nodded. "We were that eager, once. Fresh out of school, you heading to university, me doing…whatever. The world was at out feet."

"And then we learned better," I agreed. I shoved my phone in my pocket and hunched my shoulders.

"Would it be so terrible to let him play? To let the bargain come to fruition?" Baz asked. "He bargained for a shot at fame, surely we could give him that."

I sighed. "We could. But what would the Fae get out of the deal? Even if Grant is his son, there's going to be something lost in the bargain. Something bad."

"Bad enough to hurt other people," Baz said quietly, adjusting his sunglasses. "I know, I know. I've dealt with the Fae more than I would like these last few months. I know how insidious they are, how good they are at manipulating things to their favour, at grasping power. It just…doesn't seem fair."

"Life's not fair," I snapped. "She doesn't care whether this kid gets crushed by his dreams or by a bargain with the Fae, so long as things are interesting. We keep him from playing and the bargain is over. No power struggle for the Fae, no price exacted from

Grant, everyone wins. The kid will just have to learn to adjust his dreams. As we all did."

"And look at how that turned out," Baz growled. "What happy, hopeful people we are."

I said nothing to that. What was there to say? I'd literally been slaughtered what felt like hundreds of times in the last few years, each time experiencing the pain of that death while returning moments later. My soul had been on the run for five hundred years, terrified and tortured. I was a Reaper, who enforced the choices people made without question. Yes, I had happy moments. I had my girlfriend, Neja, and my friends Agravane and Yolanda, and so many others. I had my pet griffin ghost, Tempest. I had my mother and Baz. I had a life. A good one.

I also had pain.

I knew what it felt like to have dreams crushed beneath the heel of an indifferent power. Unfortunately for Grant, though, this was the best option to save lives and prevent the Fae from getting something irretrievable.

I had to stay close and monitor the festival, but for now, I needed to make myself scarce to maintain the impression to Grant and his ever-watchful Fae that I was in a meeting. So—looking around for the other Cal —I took myself to the nearest coffee shop, ordered the largest black coffee I could manage, then sat down and called my girlfriend.

The phone didn't often work between realms, so I was pleasantly surprised when I managed to get through.

"Hey, Cal!" Neja said. There were several grunts and a yelp on the other end of the line. I held the phone away from my ear until the noise of the fight died down.

"Did I catch you at a bad time?" I asked.

"No, just tying up some loose ends on a job. Don't move, you idiot, or you'll just make the ropes tighter."

I assumed that the last part wasn't addressed at me. "I can call you back…"

"No need! I'm all done, so long as these fools wait quietly to be picked up. Just a simple prisoner retrieval for the goblins. They're not as cunning as they think. Anyways, what's up? How's the festival going? I bet Baz is thrilled that he gets to spend so much time with his favourite band."

I snorted. "He's ecstatic. It's a little frightening, actually. I've managed to pry him away from them for all of a few minutes at a time, and even then, I think he's bought out all of their merch."

"Oooh, tell him to pick up a t-shirt for me. They have the most comfortable clothes." There was a rustle and then another yelp. One of the goblins, I assumed, trying to escape. It was nice to hear such a normal situation, something so typical. Neja, being a bounty hunter, was in all sorts of scrapes, and I took a strange sense of comfort from the fact that things were continuing on as usual, even if for me they weren't.

"Cal, what's going on?" Neja asked. "You're being pensive. I can practically feel it, even over the phone."

I shrugged, then remembered she couldn't see me. Video calls only worked for about three minutes across realms, and while I really wanted to see her face, I wanted to make the conversation last. "It's just…things are weird."

"Aren't they always?" Neja snorted.

"I met the guy Death was meant to hire instead of me," I said.

Silence. A couple of people in the coffee shop gave me weird looks, but they quickly went back to their own lives, either reading or talking or scrolling through their phones. Neja, though, said nothing for a long moment.

"After all this time? It's not a coincidence, then." Her voice was cold, calculating, as if she were assessing the situation for danger.

"Not a coincidence," I replied. "He's hunting me. Wants to switch roles. Lives. I don't know how he'll manage it, but it's something to do with blood magic and—"

"Whoa, whoa. *Blood* magic?" Neja hissed. "That's highly dangerous, not to mention *illegal.*"

"I knew it was perverse, but really? Illegal?" Elsewhere and its magical citizens, even those that lived in the mortal realms, had certain codes of conduct to live by, but there were very few things that were outright banned, so long as you were powerful enough to pull it off.

"Life *and* Death outlawed it centuries ago, and the accords were ratified by the dragons, which just tells you how absolutely problematic this is. Cal, you *cannot* let this guy get your blood."

"Uh…he may already have a few drops," I admitted, then relayed the incident from the day before.

Neja cursed, loudly enough that I had to hold the phone away from my ear again. I got more strange looks from the coffee shop customers. "Okay, okay. Only a few drops? That shouldn't be so bad. But if he gets any more, then we have a serious problem. Blood magic is highly dangerous, not just for the people being manipulated by the spells, but for the sorcerer. It's messing with the fundamental rights of a being, stripping away their individuality and essentially unmaking them. It goes against Life and Death, tearing a hole into the fabric of Fate. Though, now that you've imprisoned her, it might actually be easier to perform the spells. It's just…this is really, really bad."

As if I hadn't already figured that out. "I know," I murmured.

"I mean, you're not just an average person anymore, Cal. Blood magic with you as the target will be explosive, to say the least. You're a Reaper! Not to mention you have Death's heart. And—"

"Neja, I know," I said, more firmly. "It's bad. I'll do everything in my power to prevent this from happening."

"Your power may not be enough, Cal. The Reapers, back when there were more of them, were tasked almost exclusively with destroying those who used blood magic. Then they vanished. There's only you, now. You may have to get Baz involved."

"Baz?" I frowned. "What does he have to do with this?"

"The use of blood magic goes against the laws of Elsewhere, Cal. In his official capacity as Justice, Baz might be able to do more than you can as a Reaper, no matter how powerful you are."

My stomach sank. I knew that Baz could take care of himself—mostly—but he was still family. Still relatively new to this world of magic and monsters. I didn't want him to get hurt, and certainly not on my behalf.

"Just…" Neja sighed, and suddenly I wanted her to be here, so I could bury myself in her arms and make the world go away. "Be careful, Cal."

"I will," I promised, and meant it. I might not be able to die, but there were fates worse than death.

Before I could say goodbye, there was a roar of sirens out on the street. Screams sounded, loudly enough that I could hear them from inside the coffee shop. I ran outside, abandoning my coffee, and found myself gaping at a plume of smoke reaching into the sky. It was coming from the music festival.

CHAPTER 11

Given the massive number of emergency vehicles in the parking lot, it was easy to slip back into the festival without anyone the wiser. Of course, the majority of people were running *away* from the large plume of smoke, so I did get a few weird looks as I ran in with my designer clothes and distinct lack of emergency gear, but most people ignored me completely. Avoiding detection was perfectly fine with me. Especially with Other Cal on the loose.

The fire was contained to one of the stages, though the entire stage structure was consumed by eager flames. Any instruments and equipment were a total loss. Firefighters shouted at each other and sprayed water on the fire, but as far as I could tell, nothing was happening. That was probably bad.

A few paramedics hovered over a group of people that had managed to stagger away from the flames. I recognised Ferris and Baz arguing with one of the paramedics, Ferris waving her arms about in a fairly agitated manner, Baz scowling with his arms crossed. Behind them, Valerie was standing over a couple of people, muttering while she moved her hands through the air. After a moment, I realised I recognised the people on the ground, too.

The band.

Alice was walking nervously nearby, her hands fiddling with every bit of jewellery she had. Bertie kept close to her, watching warily. Jacques leaned against one of the ambulances. Richard was sitting on the ground, head in his hands. Steve, though, looked like he had caught the worst of it; he held a bloody piece of gauze to his head, face smeared with soot.

I approached carefully, not entirely sure what I was going to find.

"Ma'am, I appreciate that you need to interrogate these people, figure out what happened, but if we don't get them to the hospital soon, then the smoke inhalation could be severe." One of the paramedics, a tiny woman with an intense expression, glared up at Agent Ferris.

"I'm fine," Richard protested, sounding more gravelly than usual.

"What's going on?" I asked as I approached. The paramedic turned on me with fire in her eyes.

"Sir, step back. This is for official personnel only and—"

"He's fine," Steve said. "Family."

Three whole words out of Steve. Something must have gone severely wrong in my short absence.

The paramedic looked at me skeptically, but I must have borne enough of a familial resemblance—or was unassuming enough—to be waved through. She went back to arguing with Ferris while I crouched down next to the band members. Bertie and Alice shuffled closer, while Jacques hovered protectively.

"What happened?"

"We were keeping an eye on things, like you said, helping out with some of the roadies—not Grant—and Richard spotted a fire starting under the stage." Alice was talking so quickly that it was difficult to understand her. Adrenaline probably.

"Under the stage?" I frowned. That was where our countercurses were.

Alice nodded manically. "It was fine one minute, then poof! The electrical equipment just caught fire, lighting the boards, and by the time that we cleared the area, the entire stage was engulfed. The band, a bluegrass trio, Distillery something or other, they made it out. Banjo player got burned pretty badly; he was taken to the hospital already. His leg. Steve got hit in the head when one of the light fixtures fell. Richard pulled him out."

I examined the two injured musicians, but being completely useless at things like first aid and medical skills, all I could determine was that they were awake, talking, and looking rather worse for wear. I agreed with the paramedic; they did need to get to the hospital.

"Ferris," I said, standing. The FBI agent spun and

glared at me. "Let them go. Surely you can get their statements later."

She narrowed her eyes. "And you know so much about law enforcement?"

Baz let out a pointed cough, drawing Ferris's ire. She growled something then stalked off. The paramedic snorted with satisfaction then went to work, bundling Richard and Steve into ambulances and directing the other band members with practised ease. That left Valerie, Baz, and me standing there with the aftermath of the fire behind us.

"Do you think they'll cancel the festival?" I asked, perhaps more hopeful than anything.

Baz shrugged. Valerie clicked her tongue and shook her head, hand on her trusty picnic basket. "I heard some official looking people in suits talking about it, but it doesn't look promising. Apparently the cost of cancelling the festival would be more than any potential liability for keeping the festival running. They've already called electricians to come out and make sure that the rest of the stages are all wired correctly before tomorrow."

"Surely the authorities wouldn't let it keep going. I mean, even I know that America is a litigious society. Someone's going to sue." Though, humans were a strangely adaptable bunch, not nearly as afraid of danger as they should be. Look at me, what sort of messes I managed to get into. And I was not only sensible, but English.

"It's the Fae spell," Baz grumbled. "Any sane person would cancel the festival. There's no reason to keep it open. Attendees won't come unless they're stupid. But the gates will stay open. Your contest is only pushing matters."

I flinched. He was probably right. The Fae bargain was doing everything it could to get the other bands out of the way so Grant could step in and have a chance at fame and glory. The fire eliminated the bluegrass trio, and while it would have normally shuttered things, the magic of the bargain was keeping the festival running. My contest, offering marketing to the winner, would force the festival to its conclusion, if only to give Grant a chance.

"I could cancel it," I offered.

"The spell would only find another way to give Grant what he wants," Valerie said, patting my arm. "But you already knew that."

I did. I turned to my cousin. "What do you think?"

"People are getting hurt. Not just a little bit, but a lot. A fire like this is much worse than anything that's happened so far. It's dangerous, Cal," Baz said. He let out a huff, full of anger. "I can't just walk away anymore. We stop the bargain, great. But Grant is going to have to face the consequences of his actions just as much as the Faerie is."

I winced, but there wasn't anything I could do. This was Baz acting in his role as Justice. Things like this happened all the time and generally, it was just the way things were in Elsewhere, but when it happened right in front of Baz, he literally could not look away. Whatever magic had made him Justice bound him to certain rules. Just as I was bound to my

Reaper duties. Just as we were all bound in some form or another.

We waited until the fire was completely out before heading back to the hotel. Ferris stopped by the hospital on the way, muttering something about having to interview the band. I was mentally preparing to order room service as soon as I walked into the hotel doors, but all of that came to a grinding halt when I saw who was waiting for me at the entrance.

"Mr. Keeling," I said. "What are you doing here?"

Grant at least had the grace to blush and avert his gaze, scuffing his shoe against the street. He clutched his guitar case in his hand. "Well, I, uh…that is, I wanted to make sure that you got out of the festival alright. With the fire and everything."

"That is thoughtful of you, but an email would have sufficed." I fixed him with my best disapproving stare, and a hint of Reaper ability rumbled to the surface, brought on by my own anger at the kid's idiocy. "Coming to my hotel, on the other hand…"

Grant flinched, taking a slight step backwards. "I, uh, thought that maybe if you saw me—"

"What, if I saw you perform then I would immediately agree to promote you? Market for you? The world doesn't work like that anymore, if it ever did." I knew I was being harsh, cold, even a bit cruel, but as Baz had stated earlier, this was more than a few incidents. People were seriously injured, and though he was not the one wielding the magic, it was at his behest.

"I'm good. Really good," Grant croaked, and I

thought I saw silver limning his eyes before he blinked it away.

My Reaper magic built up, the edges of my vision losing their colour. Baz put a hand on my elbow, squeezing hard, enough to break me out of the haze. Grant was staring at me, wide-eyed with fear. I didn't know what he'd seen, but I decided it was time to stop playing ignorant. To stop playing games.

"Are you good enough to make it on your own?" I demanded. "Or are you always going to depend on the Fae, selling away pieces of your soul before each performance? Oh, I see! Was the price something different? Another human sacrifice, a changeling? Or the power that glory and fame would afford?"

"How do you know about—"

"We are not fools," Baz hissed, and this time it was me holding him back, hand wrapped around his wrist. "We know the curse that has laid the festival low."

"That wasn't me!" Grant insisted. "He—"

"Is only performing magic at the behest of your bargain," Baz snarled. "Those injuries tonight? The ruination of property? That may not have been you wielding the sword, but it was at your direction."

Grant backed up until he was against the wall, his guitar still clutched in his hands. "You don't understand! How hard it is to fit in with the rest of the world when you're like me. People don't see me. Or they actively avoid me. How can I get a fair chance when the odds are stacked against me? My father is only making things better for me!"

"At what cost?" I asked darkly.

Grant paled.

"There is always a price for these things, Grant Keeling. Best you learn that now, while it can still be undone. Break your bargain with him. Release the curse."

"I *can't*," Grant breathed. "The bargain was sworn. And…even if I could, I wouldn't. It's worth it!"

"Is it?" I raised my brows and curled my lip. "The injury of other musicians is worth it? The destruction of property is worth it? What else is worth it? The death of innocent bystanders? The loss of free will for those that listen to your music? What price did you pay for your own selfish dreams?"

"It's not selfish to dream," Grant snapped. He was truly crying, now, and any passerby would likely take one look at the situation and step in. Baz and I were older, obviously richer, and Grant was far too compelling to ignore, even if he were a changeling.

"No," Baz said, trying to gentle his tone, though I could hear the underlayment of anger. "It's not selfish to dream. It *is* selfish to act on it at the expense of others. What price, Grant?"

He licked his lips, eyes darting to either side, searching for an escape. I let my Reaper abilities rise up a bit more, let him see the depths that lurked in me. I could hear both my hearts beating louder as my magic rose. Grant shrank just a bit more.

"The tears of my audience," he murmured. Then, straightening with the arrogance of youth. "But that's nothing! Who cares about tears? It's not like people *want* to cry."

"Crying releases pent up emotion," Baz snarled, stepping closer. "It let's people feel sadness, anger, grief. Tears of joy, tears of pain. Without them, what will people have?"

"Happiness!" Grant insisted. "People will be happy!"

"Or will they feel anything at all?" I could see a few people coming closer, drawn in by our argument. I straightened my sleeves and glared at Grant. "Call off the bargain."

"I can't. I told you that already," Grant snapped.

"Very well. Then I will do everything in my power to prevent you from ever playing at that festival." I met his gaze, so he could see precisely how serious I was.

"And for all those who are injured, for all that is lost or destroyed at the hand of your father's magic, I will be there, taking account." Baz sounded downright ominous; I was surprised Grant didn't run away. Instead, he tightened his grip on his guitar case.

"I deserve this. You don't understand," he hissed. Then, he slipped away, back up and rage radiating off of him, enough so that people kept their distance.

I deflated. "This is bad, Baz. The bargain is sworn, which means breaking it could involve killing Grant. And even if he could break it, he won't, not now."

"Yeah, maybe provoking him wasn't our best plan." Baz sighed, drawing a hand through his hair. "But the festival is closed for the night anyways."

"We need a better way to counteract the Fae spell."

"Call Valerie?"

I nodded. "Yep. Call Valerie."

CHAPTER 12

Valerie shovelled some Thai food into her mouth, speaking around what looked like beef. "You called me for help with a curse, and now you want my help with Faeries?" She swallowed. I winced, handing he a napkin. Valerie smiled. "I should start charging for my services."

"We will, of course, pay you," Baz said, somehow less concerned about her eating. Probably because he, too, was shovelling food into his mouth without concern for the rest of us.

I've been told that I'm a bit stuffy. On occasion. I have a hard time believing it when faced with the lack of manners that most of the world presents.

"Seems to me you have it figured out," Valerie said. "The curse cannot be broken, not before the end of the festival in any case. Not without killing Grant. But if it goes any further, then the people at the festival are in serious danger. We have another day and a half of keeping people safe, and no countercurse is going to be able to handle that. At least, nothing that someone like me can perform. You need a real witch, one from your neck of the woods. Which, I'm assuming if you had access to, you would have contacted before talking with me."

Her expression turned sympathetic. Sad, even. But there were unspoken words that lay between us and I didn't want to be the one who spoke them and made them real.

"What if we just get Keeling out of the way?" Ferris asked. She had joined us, reluctantly, after taking the band's statements at the hospital, demanding large amounts of food as recompense.

"And which of us will kill him?" I asked, a bit of Reaper filling my tone. Ferris, though, being perfectly human—and scary enough on her own besides—just scoffed.

"I'm sure you've killed plenty, Mr. Thorpe. But, no, I was just thinking we get him out of the way. There was a fire at the festival, after all. I could probably arrest him on charges of arson." Ferris shrugged.

I gaped at the FBI agent. Baz did, too, though he did it with a mouthful of noodles. Could it be that simple? Truly?

"You can do that?" Baz asked, words barely intelligible. He swallowed hurriedly. "You can really do that? Arrest him? Keep him locked up until the festival is over?"

Ferris shrugged. "I don't see why not. It takes ages to investigate arson. All that forensic work with accelerants and such. Besides, it's the weekend. No judge will see him until Monday, which means no bail. He'll be in lockup at least until then. And the festival ends on Sunday. So…"

I could have kissed her. Baz looked like he thought the same, something between awe and infatuation flitting across his face--though most of it was thankfully hidden by his sunglasses; I didn't need to see what a disaster it would be if Ferris realised about Baz's crush on her. She was scary enough.

"Do that," I said. She glowered at me. "Please. Please do that immediately."

"What about the bargain?" Valerie asked. "Won't it try to interfere?"

"Probably," I admitted, then waved off the concern. "Truly, though, what can a Fae bargain do against the mortal legal system? It's got its own special brand of magic that is nearly impossible to understand."

"What about the festival, though?" Valerie asked. "The people there?"

"They'll be considerably safer with Grant out of the way and not actively trying to steal their spotlight than if we just let him run around and put out fires as he goes." Baz stabbed his dinner with considerably more gusto than was typical, and he smiled as he did it.

Details were hashed out, but to me, it was solid. I knew the Fae magic would retaliate, but hopefully it would be against Grant. I didn't want the kid hurt, not really. If he was stupid enough to make bargains like that, though, then there was little I could do to interfere. A bargain sworn demanded payment one way or another, and either Grant or his Faerie father would have to pay. As long as it wasn't innocent bystanders, then I was okay with that.

Well, mostly okay with that.

Ferris left, talking on the phone and supposedly issuing arrest warrants or whatever it was that actually happened in this sort of situation. I had spent too much time watching cop soap operas with Yolanda and Agravane to know how things really worked. Baz and Valerie and I finished up our dinner, chatting merrily about what we would do once the curse was broken and the festival over. Valerie had her garden, I had my marketing, and Baz would, well, do something.

It all felt easy. Too easy. And even as I thought it while brushing my teeth, I knew that it was true. Arresting Grant would only make the game more difficult. Still, it was worth a try.

I got the text message from Ferris about a quarter to midnight: *It's done.*

Instead of a weight lifting from my shoulders, though, it settled in deeper. I didn't even try to sleep, knowing that I would likely dream of Fae and bargains and magic. It turns out that was a very, very good thing. Because at approximately two in the morning, someone snuck into my room and tried to murder me.

They weren't terribly subtle.

The door swung open with the distinctive click of hotel doors, revealing a large patch of light from the hallway. I was sitting at the table, a cup of weak coffee in front of me, hunched over my phone. I should have been doing some marketing work, since I was backed up from this whole "save us from this terrible curse" nonsense. Instead, I was playing a game. The cheerful, repetitive music was a strange counterpoint to the person who rushed at me with knife in hand.

Now, in times past, it would have been a matter of ease for whoever wished to kill me to pull it off. I had been—and generally still was—completely useless at fighting of any sort. But since the return of my soul, my self-defence skills had improved. Marginally.

That is to say: instead of dying within moments, I managed to flail about and get in a few good blows to my attacker while receiving only slight knife wounds on my arms as a result. I scrambled away from the table, my phone dropping to the floor and playing that horrid music. The dim light from the one lamp I'd left on was enough to illuminate my attacker.

"You are more foolish than I thought," the other Cal Thorp growled. He was wearing black slacks and a white shirt with a shiny name tag, likely some approximation of the hotel uniform. It had been enough to get him into my room, it would seem. He twirled the knife expertly between his fingers, looking far more like a movie villain than I ever would. The flare of jealousy in me at that thought was completely irrational. "Even after I threatened you, here you are. Without ward or guards. Do you not fear death? I mean, I know you work for him, but surely you are still afraid of him? Of dying?"

I realised something very significant in that moment. The other Cal Thorp didn't know that I couldn't die. He didn't know that I was a Reaper, that I had Death's own heart beating next to my own, that I'd died a thousand times and felt the pain of every one of them, only to return, unscathed. He thought I was still human.

"Look," I said, raising my hands in some semblance of a defensive stance. "Surely we can work something out. I'll call Death—or Life, even!—and we'll restore you to the fate of the world. It will all—"

"Work out?" Cal sneered. He took a single, menacing step forwards. My vision started to lose some of its colour, a sign of the Reaper part of me rising to the surface. "You must think I'm a complete idiot to trust the word of someone like *you*. Cal Thorpe, marketing agent to the world of magic. Yet no one sees you like I do. Thief. Weak. You can't even fight me off."

Well, if we had swords that would be a different matter. My soul was an expert in swordsmanship, and I had picked up enough of his memories to pull it off. (Just don't ask me how, because I don't really know.) But in that moment, there would be no way I could fight off a vengeful doppelganger.

"I'll swear it," I said, holding my hands up.

"It isn't enough," Cal snarled. He lunged for me, knife gleaming. I raised my arms to cover my head and felt the bite of steel into my right arm. Before I could do something intelligent, like run, Cal started chanting. Blood flowed from my open wound, twining through the air. I realised too late that he was collecting it, trapping it in a vial that was big enough to furnish whatever blood magic he had in mind. I started fighting in earnest, then.

With a yowl, I leaped for the vial, tipping it over until it spilled onto the floor. Whatever spell Cal had been chanting got cut off as I barrelled into him, bringing us both to the floor. From there, it was a matter of wrestling for control. We were pretty evenly matched, physically speaking, being about the same size. I could easily have dipped into my Reaper abilities and subdued him with a quick flare of magic, but a part of me wanted to keep that particular talent quiet.

Of course, in my enthusiasm, I had forgotten about the knife. Other Cal brought it up in a quick thrust, digging the blade deep into my side. I was too shocked to scream, instead scrambling backwards and clutching the wound. It was bleeding a lot. Enough that I could feel the life draining out of me. Death's heart began beating louder, filling my ears. White began crowding the edge of my vision.

Cal leaned over and held his vial below my bleeding wound; I was too weak to stop him, though I batted ineffectually at his hand. He leered at me as he straightened, putting cork to vial and tucking it away in his pocket.

"This will be so much easier when you're dead," he purred, wiping his bloody hands on his shirt, seeming not to care that it carried evidence of a pretty serious crime. Before I could say anything, even in snark, he left.

The door hardly clicked shut behind him when my death caught up with me. My vision turned fully white, and reality vanished from around me. I hadn't seen this place since before I was reunited with my soul; since then, my deaths had been so quick as to only cause me to be out for a moment. Now, though, instead of an impossibly empty plane, so bright it was hard to look at, there were shadows there.

Find us, they said, voices so unique as to blend together in a choir. They sounded like they were in agony.

I opened my mouth to ask questions, to say something—anything—and crashed back into my body. My wounds were healed, my clothes were ruined, and my phone lay on the floor a few feet away, screen cracked. We must have rolled over it in the fight.

I like to believe that I'm a generally even-tempered sort of guy, barring the last few weeks after reuniting with my soul. But seeing the broken carcass of my phone moments after having my blood stolen by a man who could have easily been me had things gone differently, broke whatever tenuous control I had over my temper.

The Reaper magic I bore took control. My sight became greyscale; the spots of blood on the floor were more void than shadow. My skin sloughed away, my bones shattered and reformed, and I emerged from myself as a riot of darkness. I writhed in serpentine coils, maw full of fangs, talons on my feet. The room was too small, so I pushed towards the window.

"Cal!" A shout behind me.

I turned and saw a figure there, body shaped like a human, glowing with the power of an Ancient. His eyes were empty even as his hands were full of strength. Justice. Baz.

"Cal, maybe take a deep breath," Baz said, holding out those power-filled hands to me. Supplicating.

"He stole what was mine," I snarled, my voice shaking the building. Baz winced.

"Why don't we have a nice cup of coffee and you can tell me about it?" Baz sidled towards the table where my abandoned cup still sat. Gingerly, he sank into a chair. "See? This isn't so bad."

I growled deep in my throat.

"Come on, cousin. Take a breath, have some coffee. Breathe with me. In. Out. In. Out."

I snorted, my rage quavering slightly at the absurdity of this creature before me. Even with the power of an Ancient bound to his bones, he was no match for me. For the In Between, for he who stood between Life and Death. Yet I knew this man. And I breathed.

In. Out. Just as he asked.

Slowly, my form collapsed, shadows writhing in on themselves until they merely floated around me in a halo of night. My talons became fingers, my fangs nothing more than human teeth. My vision returned to colour, though grey lurked at the edges of my eyes.

I sat.

Baz let out a low sigh of relief, shoulders slumping. "So. What happened?"

"The imposter stole my blood," I snarled, shadows manifesting around my fist as I slammed it into the table. The coffee cup shattered into a thousand pieces.

Baz paled. "The other Cal? He was here? How much did he get?"

"Enough."

"And he can do what he…what he claims?"

I curled my lip, watching my darkness spread around the room, licking up every last drop of my blood. "He will try. The consequences will be vast."

I would stop him before he could complete his spell. And then he would see the full measure of my power.

But first, I needed to find him. I turned to Baz.

"I need to borrow your phone."

CHAPTER 13

"I could have handled it," Baz grumbled under his breath. It was early morning; the music festival hadn't yet opened for the day and it was chilly enough that I wondered if many people would even come. Though, with Fae magic egging them on, I had a feeling it would be a full crowd.

"We don't even know where he is," I said, sighing into my coffee. My Reaper powers hadn't quite fallen asleep since my attempted murder, since the Other Cal stole my blood. I was on edge, waiting for the blood magic to take effect at any moment. "Besides, we have to be here to—"

"This sorcerer is far more important than a Fae bargain," Baz snapped. He pinched his nose, rubbing where the sunglasses sat. "That's not entirely accurate, perhaps. Still, I know I could do more trying to catch that bastard than I could here."

"And again, I say that we don't even know where he is."

"Cal's right, Baz." A short, lean woman walked up to us, as if emerging from the morning mist, though I knew better. Neja, her greyish-blue skin mostly covered in leather, white hair tied tightly in a braid, had a sword over one shoulder, a holster with a gun on her left hip, three throwing knives on her right hip, and a thigh sheath with a wicked-looking dagger hilt showing. I knew that she was only displaying a small percentage of her arsenal, and while the mortals would likely take issue with her weapons, I was glad of them.

Before I could stop myself, I had practically thrown my coffee at Baz and wrapped my arms around Neja. She tensed for a brief moment then melted, her arms going around my waist, nose burying into the base of my neck. She smelled of jasmine and leather and violence.

"I missed you," I murmured, feeling more emotional than I had been over the last few days. I was about to cry, if my blurry vision was any indication.

"I missed you, too," Neja said, just as quietly. Then she pulled back and hit me in the arm. Twice. "You always get into trouble when I'm gone!"

"I didn't mean to!" I protested. Baz snorted, taking a sip of my coffee.

"I still think—"

"Trust me, Baz," Neja said, hands on her hips, "whatever you think you can accomplish, I can do it faster. You might have the power in your role as Justice, but I know how to hunt down people who don't want to be found. Fast. And it sounds like you need this done fast."

I nodded. I didn't know how long it took to prepare or perform a blood magic spell, but the Other Cal—or perhaps I should call him Evil Cal—had been in possession of my blood for nearly five hours, now. I hadn't felt any desire to do something untoward, but who knew how these things happened?

"You catch him, and you bring him to me," Baz growled. "Understood?"

"He stole Cal's blood, not yours," Neja countered. She jerked her chin at me. "He's a Reaper. He can take care of it."

I frowned. I wanted to ask what that meant, but I knew full well. Evil Cal had broken the laws of Elsewhere. As a Reaper, I would have to hunt him down and eliminate him for violating the free will of an individual, depriving them of their choices. It was, after all, what I was meant to do: stand between Life and Death at the crossroads, offering a choice, and defending the right to make that choice. I had no definitive proof that Evil Cal had performed blood magic before, but given that he was confident enough to go after *me* then there was little doubt.

Even if he didn't know I was a Reaper, bore Death's heart, couldn't die, then he had to know I was protected by Life and Death's favour. You didn't take on that sort of favour without practise.

"He has broken laws. He has violated the primary rules of Justice," Baz said in a low voice. "I have as much right to him as Cal."

For a brief moment, I thought I saw a flicker of gold emanating from Baz. I thought of what I'd seen when in full Reaper form, the power of an Ancient being that was fused to his very soul. It was difficult seeing my cousin, by all accounts a laid back sort of guy, with such power. Such determination for the kill.

Then I remembered that the Justice before Baz—whom I had inadvertently caused to be killed—had been an assassin.

"How about I catch him, then you and Cal can flip a coin?" Neja said. She didn't wait for an answer, just pressed a quick kiss to my cheek then walked away. A glamour fell over her even as she moved; by the time she reached the corner, she looked like a biker in full leather, blonde hair streaming behind her. Fierce. But ultimately ordinary.

"Careful," I breathed.

Baz grumbled out a series of rude words. Then, finishing my coffee, he threw it in the bin and shuffled towards the festival gates. We waited a few minutes more and were greeted by Valerie and Steve, the former smiling widely and the latter looking as if we'd dragged him out of bed by his toenails.

Valerie handed each of us a large piece of chalk before we could even get polite greetings out of the way. "Now, these are as powerful as I could get on such short notice, which is to say, not very. But they'll work to renew the countercurse, enough that they should last the rest of the day and we'll have no more fires."

Baz scowled at his chalk. "Is this even necessary since Grant's been arrested?"

Valerie's smile diminished somewhat. "Oh, well. Ah,

apparently there was some sort of mixup with the paperwork. He was released this morning."

"What?" My Reaper magic started roiling again, and I was already having a difficult time trying to control it. Hearing that Grant was out and about only made things worse.

"I heard about it through Jacques, who heard about it through Alice, who got it from a nurse at the hospital. Apparently it was big news since he was arrested for arson." Valerie clicked her tongue, shaking her head. "It was a good try, but that Faerie magic must be very powerful to move so quickly, especially on a weekend."

I'd been counting on the ridiculous complexity of the mortal—and American at that—legal system being strong enough to do battle with Fae magic. Apparently I was wrong.

"That means things are only going to get more dangerous," I said. "We need to be on our guard. Renew the countercurses after each set, if necessary."

Steve shook his head. "Officials are nervous about the fire. They're cancelling tomorrow. Only today. And only one stage. Big band happening this evening."

It was the most I'd ever heard Steve say, and even that felt cryptic and confusing. But what I could parse was that the festival had cancelled tomorrow's activities because of the fire. I had a feeling that if the magic hadn't been in effect, the entire festival would have been closed. What I didn't understand was the statements about only one stage and the big band. I hadn't thought there was much in the way of jazz at this festival.

"They're bringing in the headliner early," Baz translated for me. "And reducing performances to the one stage. It will mean fewer places to watch, but the magic will be concentrated there. It'll be easier for Grant to get his chance."

"He only needs one song," I said, nodding agreement. Three minutes out of a whole day? Relatively easy.

I cursed. This day was not turning out how I had hoped. This whole affair was not turning out how I had hoped. I hated Chicago. Bad things kept happening to me here.

"How is everyone else?" I asked Steve. He scowled and scuffed his shoe on the ground.

Valerie let out a dramatic, heartfelt sigh. "*Such* a shame. Smoke inhalation, the doctors say. Bad enough to keep them in the hospital for another day, waiting on tests to make sure that there wasn't any lung damage. Steve here only got out because, well, he put a spell on the head nurse. Don't worry, though, everyone will be fine! They just, er, won't be performing for another month or so."

As much as I disliked the Tiny Dinosaur with Phasers music, I had to feel a little badly for the band.

"I'm sorry," I said to Steve, who shrugged.

"That leaves..." Baz did some scanning on his phone, likely looking over the festival social media. He frowned. "That can't be right. There are only two bands performing today. Plus the headliner, but they're not going on until later in the evening. That's not enough to last the whole day."

Leaving plenty of time for Grant to get his show in.

Whoever this Faerie was, he had a lot of power to be able to pull of such a feat. This affected a lot of people; it wasn't some simple mental manipulation either. This was causing effects in the physical world as well as doing a number on some people's minds to organise affairs just right. I didn't pretend to be overly familiar with Fae hierarchy, but I'd spent time in the two primary courts—Winter and Summer—and hadn't seen this particular Faerie there.

"Who is this guy?" I asked, not really expecting an answer.

"Why, the Shadow King, of course."

I turned. Valerie and Steve turned. Baz turned.

Sashaying towards us in a perfectly tailored pure-black suit that had me the tiniest bit jealous, his features too beautiful to be human, eyes a little too bright to be ignored, was the Faerie who had stepped into my dreams. At his side, in a suit that was almost (but not quite) as nice as his father's, was Grant, guitar case in hand. He glared at me with all the impotent fury of a pawn in a game he didn't understand.

"I should probably know who that is," I muttered to Baz.

"Sort of an in-between to the Fae courts," Baz muttered back. "Not really part of any one court, but in communication with them all."

"Oh. Got it. A Faerie fixer."

The Shadow King scowled at me. "What an inexact and inelegant description."

I shrugged. "Give me a better one, then."

The Faerie opened his mouth, paused, considered, scowled again. "It is accurate enough for now."

Grant let out an irritated sound as he glared harder at me. "Stop trying to play games, Mr. Thorpe. You had me arrested. That's taking things too far."

"So is stealing the tears of your audience, but then you never seemed to consider the consequences of your actions when I brought up that particular issue," I replied evenly. I raised my brows at the Shadow King. "And you brought Daddy with you this time. How did you manage that? The veil in Chicago isn't weak enough to allow the Fae through, and certainly not one of his power."

The Faerie grinned, showing off teeth that were more predatory than blunted. "Surely you know as well as I that there are ways of traversing the realms, if you wish to pay the price."

Ah. The Goblin Market. An everchanging market that lived between the realms, it existed as a place where one could buy anything. For the right price. There were certain beings that could traverse the realms with ease; Life and Death were two of them, though there were constrictions on their movement due to a contract I'd had them sign at the height of the Renaissance (long story). The dragons were another, though they preferred solitude (not to mention that their movement between the realms is, ah, explosive). Neja, being a bounty hunter, a djinn, and all-around clever, was capable of traversing realms with relative ease. The Fae could move through tears in the veils between realms, but only when the veil was weak enough. For a powerful Faerie like the Shadow King, there weren't any places in the mortal realm that were weak enough to allow him through. But if he went to the Goblin Market, he could buy transport. And it would seem that our Faerie had payed.

I wondered what this trip had cost him.

"Why would you risk so much for the tears of humans?" I asked. "I can't imagine travelling between realms was a cheap buy."

"He's helping me, that's all that matters!" Grant said, taking a step forwards as if forcibly inserting himself into the conversation. The Shadow King let out a sigh.

"Quiet, boy. Excuse him, he doesn't know when to hold his tongue." The Shadow King spread his hands in supplication.

"Or when to back down, it would seem," Baz mused. Morning light caught on his sunglasses, making them gleam, as if with power.

"Back down?" Grant snorted. "I deserve this so much more than most of the so-called 'talent' that is paraded about these days. They can't even play! What do a few tears matter when compared to true talent?"

"Hush!" the Faerie snapped. "You need to learn to keep quiet in the presence of your betters."

For a Fae, that meant those with more power. Despite his connection with that world, Grant obviously hadn't gotten that particular memo.

"Betters?" he scoffed. "A washed up marketing agent

who doesn't even have a social media presence and some dude in sunglasses who tries to look tougher than he is. They don't have the power to cross you, Father. Surely you can see that!"

In an instant, the Faerie had Grant by the back of the neck. He shook the changeling like you would cruelly shake an animal, bringing him closer. "A *washed up marketing agent*?! Some *dude* in sunglasses?!" The Shadow King brought Grant closer, enough that I could have reached out and hit him in the nose, if so I chose. "A Reaper! Life's Knight and Death's Own! And him—" Grant was swung to Baz, who glowered. "—The embodiment of Justice!"

The Faerie discarded Grant with another shake. The kid landed on the ground beside his guitar case, the rough concrete tearing a hole in his suit. He trembled a bit as he stood, not for fear of Baz or myself—I doubted very much that he understood what we were —but for his father.

I hated feeling sympathy for those I was meant to dislike. Grant Keeling, half-Faerie, a changeling in a world of humans, just wanted his father's love and affection. His pride. He thought that the accolades of fans for his music would bring that. That fulfilling the bargain would do that. The Fae weren't like humans, though. They didn't love in the way humans loved. They didn't value worth in the way that humans did. Grant could fulfil every one of his father's wishes, but if he so much as slipped up in common courtesy according to the Fae, then he would be cast aside.

"You have my apologies, good sirs." The Shadow

King bowed slightly, smiling. Faerie courtesy. It felt like dust on the wind. "I came all this way to see if I could persuade you to let my son complete his bargain. Perhaps we could come to some mutually beneficial arrangement."

"You wish to bargain?" I blurted out. "With me?"

Baz, to my great annoyance, started laughing.

CHAPTER 14

Frankly, I didn't see what was so funny. I looked at Valerie and Steve, who had wisely stayed out of things to this point, and they both shrugged at me with wide eyes. Baz feigned wiping a tear from beneath his sunglasses. He bared his teeth in what could loosely be called a smile.

"You want to bargain with my cousin?" he purred, the sound a dangerous challenge.

The Shadow King, however, did not look perturbed. "If he wishes to bargain, then I would not say no."

Oh, yes, make it look like I had sought this situation out. Again, before I could say anything, Baz broke in. "Why do we not simply detain Mr. Keeling here far away from the festival? Your magic may have been able to overcome the legal system, here, but I can guarantee that it will have a much more difficult time when up against, how did you describe it, Death's Own?"

As if summoned, a hint of my Reaper powers

bubbled to the surface, tingeing the edges of my sight grey. It was one thing to explode in my hotel room, alone. It was quite another to do so out on the streets of Chicago. I tamped down the magic.

"Why are you so against this?" the Shadow King asked, tilting his head. I could tell he was starting to get frustrated, but the Fae were unlikely to let such things show if they could potentially navigate a situation to their benefit.

"The loss of a person's tears?" Baz hissed. "Their emotions? Their ability to express what they feel?"

"Have you any idea the *power* there is in the tears of a mortal?" The Shadow King licked his lips as if tasting a fine wine. I was a little weirded out. I could tell that Valerie and Steve, being mortals themselves, were also a little weirded out; they took two healthy steps back, leaning in close to one another.

"Then you bargain with each person individually for their tears. You do not take them by force, without a choice." Baz had his hands clenched into fists. His jaw was clenched. He practically radiated fury.

"Indeed," I said, trying to remain even tempered, despite brimming with magic. "Such a thing not only calls for the involvement of Justice, but my own involvement. Taking away a choice is an offence I cannot ignore."

"Oh, the crime is not my own," the Shadow King said with a slight bow. "My son, Grant, made the bargain. He is the one who pays with the free will of his audience."

As one, our attention turned to Grant. He was

standing, now, still brushing dirt from his suit with the petulant air of a wounded teenager. At his father's words, he froze. Blood drained from his face.

"W-what?" he breathed.

"Surely, boy, you realise that I cannot be the one responsible for so…invasive a price," the Shadow King said. He gestured casually to Baz and myself. "There is always *someone* willing to intervene with such, hmmm, large-scale sacrifices."

"It was the price you demanded!" Grant protested, looking wildly between us.

"And it was the price upon which you agreed," the Faerie simpered. "That places culpability purely on your shoulders."

I looked at Baz, whose expression had turned sour. "He's right. The Shadow King was, perhaps, cruel for suggesting a price, but Grant agreed to it. Therefore he is responsible for collecting the price. The violation is his."

That was so unfair it was practically criminal, but Life, as I knew, wasn't fair. Baz, being Justice, was bound by strict rules. This, apparently, was one of them. My own rules were not nearly so intense, but even the Reaper magic seemed to recognise Grant as having been the one who made the choice to bargain. Who made the choice to sell the tears of his audience to the Faerie. It was, as such, his doing.

He seemed to realise this at the same moment we did. All the blood rushed from his face and his hands trembled.

"I won't play," Grant declared, shoving his guitar

case away from him so it clattered to the ground. I winced, hoping the instrument wasn't damaged. No need to ruin a perfectly good guitar, after all. "I...I'll leave the city."

The Shadow King laughed. "Do you honestly think that will work? The bargain is struck. It must be fulfilled, or there will be consequences. You must play at this festival, for an audience. Or you will suffer eternal torment at the hands of my underlings."

Jeez. This guy hadn't even bargained with Grant's life. He'd bargained eternal torment. Dad of the year, most definitely.

Grant shook his head. "I'll call a taxi. Get out of here."

"Every car you hire will fail. Every step you take in the wrong direction will be agony. And the closer we get to the end of the festival, the more you will be compelled to play." The Shadow King's voice had the ring of truth in it. I knew the Fae couldn't lie, but this felt more like predicting the future. I wanted to put a stop to it. I couldn't. The choice belonged to Grant.

If he chose to play, I would have to stop him for violating the choices of others. If he chose to walk away, he faced the price for his bargain. A cruel fate, but one of his own making.

"But—" the Shadow King turned to me again, wearing the smile of a salesman, "—if the Reaper wished to bargain for the power to stop you, then, well, what could I do?"

I glared at the Fae. "What makes you think I don't already have the power to stop him?"

He licked his lips eagerly, eyes alight with interest. "Indeed? Well, then I can provide a different service, perhaps. Something more…intriguing?"

Baz snorted. "The only things Cal wants in life are coffee and the chance to do his job without too many distractions. And he already has those in spades."

"Hey!" I protested, though he was mostly right. I didn't get to be undistracted in my marketing work nearly as much as I would like. But I did have a lifetime supply of coffee, and given that I was immortal, it was a significant amount.

The Fae huffed, nostrils flaring. "Very well, I can see you have no wish to bargain. Know this, though: I will have my prize, Reaper, whether it is the tears of mortals or eternal torment. Which one is up to you."

With that, he walked away, not sparing Grant a single backwards glance, nor paying any attention to the other people on the streets as he went. In a gust of wind, he was gone.

Grant collapsed to the ground, pawing at his guitar case and openly shaking. Had he looked up at that moment, I was certain that he would be crying. Perhaps now he would understand just how important tears were.

Baz crouched next to the kid and put his hand on Grant's shoulder. He flinched away from my cousin. His hands, almost of their own volition, fiddled with the catch on the guitar case. Grant clenched his jaw and squeezed his hands into fists, then pulled them away from the case.

"We'll help you," Baz said.

"You will?" Grant looked hopeful, more than he had since the first time I met him.

"We will?" I parroted, a little confused. "Aren't we trying to stop him?"

Baz threw my an irritated look. "What is demanded of him is hardly fair, Cal. A choice of impossibilities."

It wasn't impossible, I knew, just impossibly diffi-cult; to sacrifice yourself for the lives and wellbeing of others was a task well beyond the reach of many. I had only managed it so many times because I knew I could die and return, over and over and over again, until there were no more impossible situations to face. Grant had no such fortune.

"What do you want to do?" I asked. It was his choice. I would help him if I could, but ultimately the choice was his.

"I just wanted to play music," Grant whispered. Already, his hands reached for the guitar case. To my surprise, Steve stepped between Grant and the guitar.

"You play music because it is in your soul, not for fame and fortune," he said, hands in pockets, staring down at Grant. With his punk regalia, he looked quite intimidating. Enough so that Grant shrank back. "This bargain, that is for fame and fortune, not music."

Grant flinched. Hunched his shoulders. Nodded. "Yeah."

Steve crouched down, his face inches from Grant's, his expression both thunderous and questioning at the same time. "Do you want to play music, or be famous?"

"I can't play music with no money," Grant breathed,

eyes filling again. "I want to play for people, not just in my garage. I want to do more than just bar gigs and—"

"Do you want to play music? Or do you want to be famous?" Steve repeated, and this time I didn't doubt that he would get a true answer from Grant.

"I want to play music." It was a breath as much as a confession. He looked up at me. "Please, help me! I thought that if I made the bargain, it would mean I could just keep playing. I didn't think that...my father, he...I don't want to be tortured for eternity." Grant broke down into a gurgling sob.

"We'll help," Baz said. He shot me a look that, even behind the sunglasses, I could tell was firm and unassailable.

"Yeah," I agreed, though I had no idea how to pull such a thing off. "We'll help."

Grant moved faster than I expected, leaping off the ground and wrapping his arms around me in a hug tight enough to cut off my air. "Thank you! Thank you! I swear you won't regret this!"

I managed a wheeze in response.

Of course, as luck would have it, a dark sedan—obviously belonging to the government—pulled up and Special Agent Ferris climbed out, fury written in every line on her face. She got one look at Grant, hugging the air out of my lungs, with Baz, Valerie, and Steve standing casually by, and froze. Her hand went to her gun.

"Cal?" Ferris snarled. "What are you doing?"

I squeaked, more from lack of air than fear of Ferris. Grant sprang back, that fear back in his eyes. He looked between the FBI agent and me, then took a step backwards. "Baz, explain," I coughed, waving my cousin forward.

Baz explained, though Ferris didn't appear to like the explanation. She glared at Grant the whole time, resting her hand casually—if such a thing is possible—on her holster. When Baz was done, she asked with a fair amount of acid, "And how, *exactly*, are you going to help him?"

"We…hadn't gotten that far?" I said.

Ferris snorted. "Of course you hadn't."

"The way I see it," Valerie cut in, still remarkably cheerful, "is that we have two courses before us. One, either Mr. Keeling fulfils his bargain with that horrid Faerie, thereby stealing the tears of his audience. Or, two, he is prevented from playing and ends up in the hands of the Fae for eternity. As Mr. Keeling has said he doesn't want to be tortured, then all we need to do is figure out how to get him to perform without anyone being hurt."

"Oh, is that all?" Ferris snapped. "Cal, this is ridiculous. Just let me lock the kid up again. The festival ends this evening. Half the ticket holders have cancelled, there are only a couple of bands left, surely—"

"Wait." I held up my hand.

Ferris sighed, folding her arms and tapping her foot, the perfect image of impatience.

"The ticket holders have cancelled," I said. Ferris nodded.

"Yeah, once you removed that contest, citing unsafe and unfair conditions—the only good thing to come out of that fire, I think—about half of the people who had been reserved for today demanded refunds from the company. I have to hold an investigation on ticket fraud and money laundering, just from the sheer number of cancellations alone."

I hadn't actually removed the contest post, and couldn't now because my phone was broken, but I knew that Yolanda and Agravane back in Elsewhere both had access to my accounts. Neja probably told them to cancel the contest when I called her. I was suddenly very grateful for my extremely smart, extremely capable girlfriend. But contest aside, Ferris had given me an idea.

I turned to Grant. "Your bargain stipulates that it's the tears of mortals your father wants, right? Does it stipulate who your audience has to be, though?"

Grant frowned. Considered. Twitched a finger in the direction of his guitar case, which was still being guarded by Steve. "I don't think so," he said at last.

"Be precise," Baz growled. "This doesn't work if you aren't precise."

Grant finally shook his head. "No. Just that the mortal tears of my audience were to be payment."

"Good." I nodded firmly. The mortal tears, not the tears of mortals. This could work. "Then I'll be your audience. And Baz."

Grant paled and took a step back. "You can't! You said it yourself that losing your tears would—"

"I'm not mortal," I said. Ferris didn't even blink, and Valerie and Steve were already fully aware of this fact.

Grant, though, frowned. "Not even a little bit," I continued. "Neither is Baz."

Well, Baz was a smidge more mortal than me, but only because he could be killed if someone tried really, really, really hard. There weren't many in Elsewhere that could pull that off, and I was certain that Grant couldn't, either, no matter how bad his music might turn out to be.

"Yeah, okay, let's do it." The young musician turned and started for the festival gates. Ferris snatched the back of his collar before he could, dragging him backwards.

"Oh, no you don't. Not until we've cleared out any other potential listeners. You get to stay with me until we do. Got it?" With that, she snapped handcuffs around Grant's wrist, then cuffed him to her.

Now I just had to figure out how to close down a festival without anyone being suspicious or getting hurt. A festival that was being kept open by Fae magic. Figures.

CHAPTER 15

Have you any idea how difficult it is to herd people away from a music festival when there is magic that literally draws them in? Even with half of the tickets for the final day being refunded or cancelled or whatever, there was a considerable number of people wandering around, waiting for the bands to start playing.

Steve had a firm hold on Grant's guitar, and the musician kept tugging at his handcuffs, much to the irritation of Agent Ferris. Baz, Valerie and I seemed almost sane in comparison, not that it helped us convince people to leave.

"Health code violation?" A young couple holding bottles of water and a funnel cake on a paper plate stared at us. They looked skeptical.

"Yes," I said. I shook my head and sighed. "Apparently, there was a massive nest of cockroaches found in the storage area for all the food vendors' carts this morning. They swarmed over everything. We're shutting down all the food vendors on that violation alone, though I'm told there were…others."

The couple exchanged a look full of wide-eyes and gaping mouths. The funnel cake wound up in the nearest bin as they hightailed it out of the festival. By the time I made the rounds to all the food vendors and people holding purchased items, about a third of the attendees had fled. No Fae magic could counteract the basic human instinct of avoiding cockroaches.

After that, we started systematically dismantling sound gear, rendering the stages useless. A plug undone here, a speaker missing there, and suddenly half of the roadies and sound engineers were standing around, scratching their heads as they called about to see if new equipment could be found. Thanks to a company credit card—and Death's very, very large bank accounts—there was no sound gear in the Chicago area. At all.

Baz swore up and down that he could sell the gear again once we got back to Elsewhere. I hoped he was right, because I didn't have the storage for any of it and I doubted Death wanted an entire city's worth of sound gear cluttering up his house.

With most of the attendees gone, all that was left to do was to clear out the last few stragglers. For that, I borrowed Baz's phone and a park bench.

"You know, I vowed years ago to never do this," I said.

"Do what?" Ferris asked, suddenly suspicious. She jerked her arm, forcing Grant—who was leaning towards Steve on the bench nearby—to sit upright again. Baz just chuckled.

"It's not illegal," I grumbled.

"No, but it did get you kicked out of your first year communications class at university," Baz pointed out. I rolled my eyes.

"They apologised. Formally. Eventually." I opened up Baz's social media apps—vastly under-used, as my dear cousin was more or less inept at such things—and cracked my fingers. Then, I got to work.

Baz explained while everyone frowned at me, obviously confused. "See, Cal is a very good marketing agent. But he is also very good at, ah, how shall we say this...counter marketing? No, they're really more smear campaigns."

Ferris wrinkled her nose in distaste. Valerie, to my surprise, leaned in. "Like those political ads they run during election season?"

Ah, American politics. About the most cutthroat activity in the world. "Something like that. It's a little more subtle, and there's less shouting, but it works on much the same principle."

Not even bothering to disguise her interest, Valerie moved to sit next to me and watched my fingers fly across the phone screen with rapt interest. After about twenty minutes, during which time Ferris had to threaten to use her taser on Grant, I'd managed to get the headliner band to cancel and agree to put on a charity show at a different Chicago theatre. Another half-hour, and the entirety of the music world was posting and tweeting and buzzing about the shady dealings going on at this music festival. There were rumours circulating about money laundering, pictures of cockroaches on food, and people saying that the whole thing was cursed anyways because of the fire and various bands dropping out of the festival. By the time Baz brought lunch—purchased from a venue far from the festival, just in case—I had people speculating on the motives of the organisers for keeping the festival open after so many things going wrong.

I would have to find a way to get the festival organisers different jobs, because I was fairly certain that this particular festival would never, ever be put on again. Thank goodness it was only the inaugural year.

By two in the afternoon, Ferris had taken to walking around the park—which was now being cleared of equipment—with Grant so that he would stop trying to get to his guitar. Steve held on to the case with a firm determination that surprised me, even going so far as punching Grant in the nose once when the musician got a little too eager and tried to sing. Baz was chewing on the straw of his third smoothie, looking thoroughly bored. Valerie had been giving me tips while she followed the whole affair on social media. But it was, ultimately, done.

I dropped Baz's phone to the table with a clatter and stretched. "That's the end of the festival. If they're not cleared out by five, I'll eat my hat."

"That doesn't leave us much time," Baz said. "We have to get Grant to perform before the festival is officially over, or, well, eternal torment."

"I vote against eternal torment," Grant said, dabbing his nose with a napkin.

Ferris started undoing the handcuffs, though she watched me with open suspicion. "That was weirdly impressive. And terrifying. I'm sure the FBI would offer you a job if you wanted one."

"Yeah," I grumbled.

Baz snorted. "Cal was offered a job by every law office, politician, and state agency after his communications class debacle. Hence the formal apology from the university; how could they punish someone who was so obviously employable?"

"What happened?" Ferris asked.

"I started doing regular marketing and ended up working at Harcourt. And just as I was about to be promoted to vice president, I got shot. The rest is, shall we say, history."

"I thought that they didn't have guns in Britain," Valerie said, smiling.

"So did I." Rare though they were, guns weren't completely gone from my home country. As I was fully aware. I shook off memories of my first death and stretched again. "Right, now. You lot should scarper. Baz and I will stay here with Grant. Ferris, you made sure that the workers are gone for an hour?"

"Told them there was something up with the electrical system, that there was someone coming to make sure people didn't get electrocuted. They'll be back by four." That gave us two hours. I didn't think Grant would need more than a song to fulfil his bargain, but on the off chance that a full set was required, we had plenty of time.

I nodded. Steve handed me the guitar case even as Grant started moving towards it. Valerie leaned in and kissed my cheek, then linked her arm with Steve. Ferris made up the party, giving us all one last look before shaking her head and leaving.

"Very clever." I whirled. The Shadow King was standing in front of the humans, fire burning brightly in his eyes, fingers tipped with wisps of magic.

"Cal..." Ferris said, reaching for her gun.

"Don't," Baz warned, but it was too late. The Special Agent shot the Faerie in a blur of motion, her instincts and muscle memory giving her perfect aim. Only, her target wasn't human. He moved so quickly that it was impossible to see; one second he was in front of the FBI Agent, the next he was at her back, his fingers wrapped around her throat.

"You *dare* try to wield iron against me?" he snarled.

Ferris whimpered. Her gun clattered to the ground and she scrabbled against his hand, ultimately achieving nothing.

"You humans," the Faerie sneered. "You think you're so clever, blending iron into every aspect of your environment. You know nothing of old magic, or of what you stand against. You try to outwit me, to remove any mortals from the place of my son's performance? Foolish."

He squeezed harder. Ferris let out a terrified squeal, her nails gouging into the Shadow King's hand; he did not loosen his grip at all.

"Stop!" Grant shouted. He still reached for his guitar, but he pulled himself away, stuffing his hands into his pockets and trembling with effort. "I am obeying the conditions of the bargain!"

"Are you? Did I not specify that my payment was to be the mortal tears of your audience? These cannot produce mortals tears, for they lost their mortality long ago!" The Shadow King spun around so he was facing us, Ferris dangling in his grasp, struggling for breath.

"We're human," I countered.

The Fae sneered. "Humanity does not necessarily equate to mortality. Certainly not in your case." He squeezed tighter. Ferris's face began to turn splotchy.

"Baz," I muttered. "We need to put a stop to this."

"I can't act, Cal," Baz growled back, obviously furious. "She shot him first."

She had. That meant the Faerie was justified in his current action. But I wasn't Justice. I let my vision fade to grey, let what remained of my humanity slip aside, the Reaper part of me coming to the fore. Before I could so much as blink, though, Valerie took a step forwards.

"I beg your pardon," she said, somehow conveying veracity and sarcasm simultaneously. The Shadow King regarded her with a raised brow and hunger in his gaze.

"Yes, human?" he cooed. "Do you wish to bargain?"

"No." Valerie hefted her picnic basket on her arm. "But I will listen to your son's performance."

My hearts beat once in my ears, so loud that it drowned out everything else. Twice, they beat. Three times. Steve turned to Valerie, his mouth forming the word, "No," though I could not hear it. Ferris' eyes widened, her skin becoming more grey, her struggles weaker.

Baz hissed, the sound enough to shatter the spell of shock.

The Shadow King released Ferris and faced Valerie. One powerful, strong, flush with life, the other weak with hunger and desperation. Valerie was old, hunched, grey, her dark skin lined with myriad wrinkles, yet in that moment I saw the power in her. Flooding through her. The power that every immortal being in Elsewhere coveted. The power of humans. Mortals.

Ferris crawled away, picking up her gun and aiming it again at the Shadow King. Baz moved before she could fire, his own immortal magic having him at her side in an instant. "Don't," he said, already dragging her away despite her weak protests.

"Valerie," Steve murmured. The old woman smiled and reached up, patting him on the cheek.

"Don't fret, my dear," she said. "I've lived a long, full life. I have few days left, and even fewer regrets."

"This won't kill you." I wanted her to understand her choice. My voice was not entirely my own, and I knew that the Reaper had taken over, though I stood in a human skin. "You will be unable to express or feel emotion strong enough to bring you to tears. Everything will be muted. Your pain will be impossible to express. Your joy will be mere warmth, instead of the flame that consumes sadness. You will be a shade of yourself."

Valerie smiled again, sad, her eyes already brimming with tears. "I know."

"What about Jacques?" Steve asked, a desperate attempt to stop her. She just took in a deep breath, squared her shoulders, and handed over her picnic basket.

"Tell him that this is his. That everything I have is his. That I love him with all my heart and that I will still be at every performance I can. That I will never not love him, no matter what he chooses to do with his life."

Steve turned to me, eyes wide and terrified. "Do something!" he demanded. "You're some terrible immortal creature. Do something! Stop this! Save her."

I shook my head, even as Valerie put her hand on Steve's arm to try and comfort him. "I cannot. I am a Reaper, a being that stands between Life and Death. Who enforces *choice*. Valerie has made her choice. Therefore, I cannot act against it."

Steve whirled to Baz, who shook his head and said nothing. The musician turned to Valerie, who patted his arm again, still smiling softly. "It will be alright," she murmured. "I've had a good life." Once again, she extended her picnic basket.

Steve took the basket. Valerie nodded firmly and turned away from him. The Shadow King watched this with eager interest, already licking his lips at the sight of tears in Valerie's eyes. Steve started backing away, pulling the wounded Agent Ferris with him. They both looked like they wanted to stay, wanted to help, wanted to sacrifice more, but couldn't.

Sacrifice wasn't easy. Nor was walking away when your friends were left behind.

Sometimes, both were the right thing.

"You would do this willingly?" the Fae asked. "You would choose this?"

Valerie sniffed, the single action showing every ounce of her disdain for the creature before her. "To save the life of a young man who deserves better? Yes, I would choose this."

Grant reached for his guitar again, still trembling, still trying to hold himself back. I handed it over and he nearly sobbed with relief as he opened the case and pulled out the instrument, the bargain compelling him to play. "I'm sorry," he said to me. To Valerie.

"It's okay," she said. "You just play something pretty. Something happy, but not too happy. A good blues tune."

Valerie had made her choice. And as Grant started to play, the tears that fell weren't for his music—good, but not yet spectacular—but for that choice. One I knew she stood by, even as it hurt. Even as it tore away something essential.

The Shadow King stood beside her and breathed in deeply, his magic wiping away Valerie's tears as they fell. He was euphoric, ecstatic, even as Grant's blues tune turned melancholy, agonising.

Moment by moment, Valerie's strong posture relaxed just a little bit until she was almost, but not quite, as she had been. She listened to the rest of the song with mild interest and nothing more. There was no rush of magic, no declaration that things had changed, but we all knew it to be true, regardless. The bargain was complete.

The Faerie turned to me, practically brimming with power. "Now, Reaper, shall we two bargain? For the location of the others of your kind, perhaps?"

I was about to explode into shadow and tell him where, exactly, he could shove his bargain when something in me froze. I gasped, doubling over, clutching my chest. My human heart stuttered. Death's heart beat stronger. Out of sync, my vision wobbled. I fell to my knees.

There was only one thing this could be. Blood magic.

Neja had failed.

CHAPTER 16

There are a few rules to abide by when dealing with magical creatures. One of them is to not show vulnerability to those who crave power, like the Shadow King. Me falling to my knees, clutching my chest like I was having heart attack? That was showing vulnerability. And for someone like me to be vulnerable before a powerful Fae?

Yeah, bad news.

Immediately, the Faerie swooped forwards, reaching for me with fingers outstretched like claws. Generally, the Fae dealt with their opponents by means of tricks and bargains, carefully worded. They rarely attacked outright, unless you had done them some wrong. But they were opportunists, and a Reaper on the ground, gasping for breath was quite the opportunity.

With a triumphant screech, the Faerie buried his talons into my throat before anyone else could inter-vene. Grant was still trembling a bit after playing and fulfilling his bargain, his guitar clutched in his hands. Valerie watched with interest, a mild fear showing on her features. Baz, at least, tried to fight, leaping forwards with his immortal strength to fight the Shadow King directly. Unfortunately for him, he had only been possessed of immortal power for a few months. The Faerie had been powerful for centuries.

"No need to bargain after all, it would seem," he murmured in my ear.

I could feel my human heart failing. It thudded irregularly, trying to support me while the Other Cal's blood magic stole the life from me. Death's heart, on the contrary, started beating stronger. Its dark magic, born of the depths of the empty universe, flooded my body. My Reaper magic reacted with the heart's magic, and the colour drained from the world.

In one smooth motion, I grabbed the Shadow King around the wrist, forcibly pulling him from my neck. The wounds there sealed over as power flooded through me. I could see whorls of darkness floating through the air around me, and everywhere I looked, I saw the yellow-gold auras of the living. The colours, the only ones I could see, corresponded with how much life they had in them, and at the moment, the Shadow King's was becoming paler. He still had a strand of silver woven in, indicating immortality, but the longer I held his wrist, the more the silver faded.

"Indeed, you are correct," I said, my voice mixed with the dying stars at the edge of existence. "There is no need to bargain."

With a twitch, I broke the Faerie's wrist. He let out a whimper.

"Cal?" Baz asked from a few feet away. He was wiping a smear of blood from the corner of his mouth. "Are you alright?"

"I am perfectly well," I said. The dark motes swirled faster around me. I squeezed on the Faerie's broken wrist. "Now, would you care to tell me about the others? The Reapers? Or shall I take the memories from your mind as you die?"

The Faerie let out another whimper. "My lord, I was a fool. I mistakenly thought that you were laid low and—"

"Thought to take what did not belong to you." I bared my teeth at him. "I am aware of your foolishness. Well? The choice is yours."

Eyes rolling in fear, he said, "There are rumours about the Reapers of old being bound at the edge of Elsewhere, beyond the dragon lands."

"That's it?" I scoffed. My magic flared. My single working heart beat steadily. "Hardly worth the effort."

"No!" the Shadow King shouted. "There's more!" He licked his lips, eyes darting around as if he could find escape from me. Fool. "They say that they were bound by the fallen gods, the forgotten powers that roam in the gloaming. Talk with the Fisher King. He has the answers you seek."

The Fisher King. An Arthurian myth, but I had discovered that most myths held some basis in truth.

"Very well. Your answers appease me. Now leave this place and never return. From this day forth, you are marked by the Reaper, and you will know that your doom follows in your wake. Mark your days well." I released the Faerie's broken wrist and tossed him aside. My magic slowed some as I watched him crawl away, then scramble to his feet and run.

I turned to the glowing auras of the two mortals who remained. Valerie, a sickly yellow. Months left to live, at most. Was it because of her giving up her tears? I peered closer. No. A monster sat in her belly, tendrils spreading as it grew. She stared back at me, unafraid, uninterested.

Grant, glowing vibrantly gold, clutched his guitar to his chest. He watched me with the look of prey before a predator.

"You have your Fae-bought fame," I said. "You need only choose what to do with it."

"Please don't kill me," he breathed.

"I won't kill you." I shook my head and turned away, only to find a figure glowing silver before me, only tiny flecks of gold showing what he had once been. "Basil Thorpe, Justice incarnate. Or reborn, perhaps, the more accurate term."

"Reaper." His expression softened. "It's the blood magic, isn't it. What happened?"

"The sorcerer stole what remained of my humanity so that he might claim it for himself." The mere thought had my magic flaring again, those motes of darkness flitting through the air in agitation. I locked eyes with my cousin, watching the silver he bore flare as his power rose. "We will get it back."

"We don't even know how to find him," Baz pointed out, annoyingly practical.

"Where would I go to do such a thing? After all, he wanted my life, my humanity. He is me, had the world been different." My magic was still clamouring for vengeance, still roaring at the defilement, but a thought in the back of my mind spoke strongly enough for attention. Even as I thought it, Baz spoke the same thought aloud.

"Coffee," he said. "If we were hunting you, we would need to find a coffee shop."

"One emptied of its customers, so there would be secrecy and space."

"Oh, yeah, in a city full of coffee shops?" Baz scoffed, shaking his head. "Where are we going to find that?"

"It's on Fifteenth Street." This came from the changeling, the half-human musician who still clutched his guitar in gold-tinged fingers. His lifeforce pulsated bright and vibrant, so full of potential and life. In his other hand, he held out a phone. "There was a, ah, incident at the police station this morning when they were releasing me. The detective said there was some sort of social media storm about a coffee shop on Fifteenth Street, something about a gas leak, only there was no leak, and the owner was sent out of town with a ticket to a cruise trip and…well, anyways, according to Google, the shop is still closed. Maybe permanently."

Baz grinned, magic flaring. "Some days, I love the internet."

Within minutes, we had summoned a ride share.

The human driving it didn't seem to notice that two of the more powerful beings in the various realms had entered his car, only stating that Grant's guitar would have to go in the trunk. Valerie stood on the curb, looking at us dispassionately.

I paused at the door of the vehicle. "They can't come with us," I pointed out.

"I helped!" Grant complained. "I gave you the information and—"

"Take Valerie to the hospital," Baz ordered. When Grant looked like he was going to protest again, Baz angled his head so that the sunglasses reflected the morning light, an effect that was both ridiculous and effective. Grant realised who held the power in this situation and acquiesced. The ride share vanished in a blur of tires.

"Now we need a new ride."

Just as I spoke, a large, black, American made SUV pulled up to the curb; it was obviously government issued. The passenger window rolled down, revealing an angry-looking Special Agent Ferris. She gave us a once-over, frowned, and asked, "Do you need a ride somewhere, gentlemen?"

"Yes." Baz climbed into the front seat, I into the back, and we were off to go confront Evil Cal.

It turned out that Ferris had done the same thing we had; she sent Steve to the hospital and waited for us just around the corner from the festival, automatically assuming that there would be more trouble. She was, unfortunately, right.

She had also been keeping track of the situation at

the coffee shop—called Joe's Cup of Joe, which apparently served one of the highest rated cups of coffee in Chicago—and simply rolled her eyes when Baz told her that's where we were headed.

"So this guy used blood magic to steal your life," she said, cutting across traffic. My magic flared, perceiving danger. I had to hold onto it tightly, telling myself it was just driving, just traffic. Either way, the black motes were multiplying, and my hold on this bipedal, human form was waning.

"In essence, yes," I said through gritted teeth.

"And you can't just make him give it back."

"Oh, I can, but it won't involved FBI approved methods."

She turned sharply, making me slide across the seat, despite the seatbelt I wore. My fingers sprouted claws of pure shadow, which I dug into the leather seats. I hoped the car was insured. "This is like the situation with Dermot Green all over again," she muttered, referring to my last trip to Chicago.

"Yes, only this time, you know that it's a magical situation the authorities are ill equipped to handle," Baz said, giving me worried glances as I did my best to keep a firm handle on my Reaper magic. With Death's heart pouring power into me, and no human heart to counteract it, I was becoming more and more entrenched in the magic, which was dangerous for those around me. Confronting the Shadow King had only awoken it; now I was eager to fight.

We arrived at the coffee shop a few minutes later. The street outside was completely deserted, leaving

Agent Ferris plenty of room to park. As soon as I stepped from the car, I knew why the street was empty; there was a malignant reek to the air, one that was primal and oozing. It would easily unnerve anyone in the area, quietly suggesting that they be Somewhere Else.

Ferris immediately drew her gun.

"Stay here," Baz ordered. I ignored them both and walked towards the coffee shop.

"Like hell," Ferris snapped.

I opened the door. A bell tinkled, announcing my presence. There was smokey jazz playing, lulling potential customers into a sense of relaxation and comfort. The floors were wooden, well-scuffed and worn. There were tables and pieces of furniture scattered about, lending the shop an eclectic, artistic look. A coffee bar stretched along the back wall, showcasing containers with several different roasts and origins, fronted by a glass bakery case. The whole place smelled of ground coffee beans.

It was a place where I would have been happy to spend an afternoon, putting together marketing campaigns and indulging in exceptional coffee.

Now, though, it was more crime scene than coffee shop.

Blood—mine, presumably—was painted across the floor and furniture in designs that even my ignorant mind knew to be ancient and dangerous. Artefacts of bird feathers, animal skulls, rocks of various types, and bits of metal, were placed strategically on the designs.

Even with the aroma of coffee masking most of the smell, there was a reek of decay.

A form, female, lay prone in the centre of the room, her skin flayed and lifeless fingers stretching towards the entrance. I stepped over to her. It was the siren who had first captured me, taking me to the Other Cal. Dead, killed in this perverse ritual for the energy that her life supplied. Her loyalty hadn't been worth much, apparently. My Reaper magic flared again, pushing at the seams of my body, snarling at the desecration before me.

I heard the bell tinkle again. Baz and Ferris, presumably.

"This is…" Ferris trailed off, and I heard her swallow back her gore.

"Profane," Baz finished, no hint of my cousin in his words. No, he was all Justice, now. "An art that was banned for a reason."

Their voices must have drawn attention to us, because a man stepped out from the back, wiping his hands on a towel. It was the Other Cal, the Evil Cal, only…different. He was just as put together, just as good looking, just as different from me as before, and yet I felt like I was looking into a mirror at myself. He froze, the towel falling to the floor.

"You're meant to be dead," he said, and something about his voice was mine, too.

"Indeed?" I asked, my own words distorted by the Reaper magic. "Well, it would seem that a mistake has been made. I think we'd better remedy it."

CHAPTER 17

*E*vil Cal didn't wait for explanations, discussions, or even an invitation. He simply held up his hands and threw magic at me. As a sorcerer, he was apparently gifted. However, I was well beyond caring about such a simple thing as pain from being hit in the chest with magic. I was pushed back by the blow, and shadows peeled away from my skin as I stumbled. Pain burned through me, feeding my anger.

I straightened, the wound—a grievous thing that cut me to the bone—being knitted by the motes of darkness. It spread, encompassing my entire body in shadow until I was wreathed in a cloak of it. "That," I growled, "was a very foolish mistake."

"Calvin Mason Thorp," Baz said, stepping forwards, intent in every movement. "You are hereby bound for breaking the laws of Elsewhere, for practising blood magic, for desecrating the sacred nature of Life, for taking away that which made someone who they are."

"What do you know of such things?" Cal snarled,

magic already gathering at his fingers. He looked between me and Baz, almost as if deciding which of us was the bigger threat. He lifted his hands. "This was meant to be *my* life. I will have it."

Before he could lift his hands higher, slinging magic about and forcing both Baz and myself to react accordingly, a single gun shot rang out. The Other Cal's head snapped back. I roared in pain, my skull fracturing, agony burrowing through my head from front to back. My vision flared white and then black and then it went grey once more. I was still alive, still caught up in my Reaper powers, still with Death's heart beating in place of my human one.

Ferris stood there, gun in hand and aimed at Cal, but her expression was one of horror. I realised what happened; she shot him in the head, but because we were linked by his blood magic—and would be until the spell was complete—then I had taken the death. And I could not die.

Cal scrabbled at his head, screaming. A moment later, he spun towards me, breathing heavily and panicking. "What was that? What *are* you?"

"Cal?" Baz hissed under his breath. I held up a hand, still dark as the edge of the universe. Baz snapped his mouth shut, but I could tell he didn't like it. He would likely step in as soon as things became violent. They most assuredly would become violent.

"Have you never felt your death before?" I asked my doppelgänger. I took a single step forwards. He mirrored me, moving back. "Have you never felt your bones shatter? Your neck break? Your heart stop beating as it is ripped from you? Have you never drowned? Burned? Been stabbed through the eye?"

"What are you talking about?!" Cal looked left and right, as if searching for an escape.

"The mistake that Fate orchestrated which put me in place to be hired as Death's marketing agent may have been what put you in this unfortunate situation, but it is not what made *me* the right person for the job." I held out a hand, shadows swirling around it, hungry as a dying star. They reached for Cal, who stumbled over a yellow painted chair. "I am a Reaper, the last. I stand between the chaos of Life and the order of Death. I am Death's marketing agent and Life's errand boy. I have experienced hundreds of deaths that will never be mine, and I have left behind the pieces of me which made me human. I am the Keeper of Choices, the Balancing Knife. I am the being you meet at the crossroads, and right now, Calvin Mason Thorp, you are at a crossroads."

He took another step back and I followed, my pace even. It was a mistake.

Magic snapped into existence around me, merging from the various artefacts that I'd seen around the room into one continuous circle. A pentagram, inscribed in blood and covered by detritus. A summoning circle, or, in this case, a binding circle. I was trapped.

My shadows roared. My form broke apart until I was scrabbling at the edges of my binding with talons and fangs, my many coils turning and twisting against the magical cage. I could see the struggle on his face, so like my own, but breaking out of the circle would take a great deal more time than I likely had. He would easily perform his spell in the time it took me to focus my power and break through the bindings.

I screeched loudly enough to shatter glass. Agent Ferris fell to her knees, hands over her ears, gun still clutched tightly. Baz flinched, but only a little. He readjusted his sunglasses and gave me the subtlest of nods.

"I knew something had gone wrong with the initial spell," Cal said, pacing before me like a zoo animal, when I was the one trapped. Slowly, I folded my shape into humanoid form, though I was still a being of shadows and endings, of the life after a fire, sparks and emptiness. Cal sneered at me. "The magic was strong, but there was just something missing. I couldn't get access to any of your social media accounts. I still couldn't interact with the world in a normal way. It was like people were seeing a person, but it wasn't me. I knew you hadn't died, that I hadn't taken all the pieces I needed from you. I knew there had to be something else going on."

"I cannot die," I said simply. I pressed my fingers against the barrier, tiny white lights flashing as I pushed against it. "Even now, bound here, I will endure."

"Impossible," Cal scoffed. "Everything dies. I just have to figure out a way to kill you."

"And to do that, you had to kill her?" I pointed to the dead siren, whose blood must have fuelled the spell for the binding circle. There was little else that was powerful enough to keep me contained than life magic, either freely given or taken by force. "The one person who knew you? Who was loyal to you?"

Cal glared at me. "Her death wouldn't have been necessary if it weren't for you."

I pressed harder against the barrier, my fingers growing claws of darkness, focusing every ounce of power I had into breaking through. I would get there eventually, but when?

Not soon enough, apparently. Baz walked around the circle, shoes scuffing on the wooden floors, his posture deceptively relaxed. He stopped just in front of me, his back to where I was bound, facing his target. "You mistake yourself," Baz said icily. "You worried about him, when you should have been concerned with me."

"Another Reaper?" Cal scoffed.

"Justice." Baz lunged, and for the first time, I wondered if my cousin was truly there at all, or if the ancient being whose power he bore had claimed him. Just as perhaps being a Reaper had claimed me. Justice as I had first met him, when I was initially hired on by Death, had been an assassin, the embodiment of justice, with little else to distinguish him but a devotion to Life that had ultimately been his undoing. Whatever he had been before was stripped away, leaving behind an immortal being of great power and danger who might have forgotten what he once was.

I hoped I was wrong. I hoped that I simply hadn't known Justice that well. Because watching Baz, my cousin and best friend, who bore this power now? There was little of the Baz I knew.

He moved with feline grace in a dance that was some sort of martial art and battle of magic mixed together. He leaned and dodged and feinted as Cal whirled and fought with magic in his hands. Other Cal had an incantation constantly on his lips as he fought Baz, one strike blending into another. Where Baz hit, blood flowed. Where Cal hit, Baz burned. Baz was rarely hit.

"Tell me what to do."

I jumped. Ferris was leaning in towards the barrier, face pale and covered in a sheen of sweat, a fragile human in a world of predators.

"Tell me how to get you out of here."

"Break the circle," I whispered. Baz landed a kick across Cal's jaw.

"How?"

I nodded my head to what looked like a deer skull that sat at one of the points of the pentagram. In theory, if Ferris managed to break or dislodge it, the circle should shatter. I would be free. She seemed to catch my meaning, despite knowing very little about magic, and raised her gun again. Before I could stop her, warn her, she fired. The skull fragmented into a hundred pieces. Cal let out a wail of fury as he realised what happened. Baz grabbed him by the throat. And the magical recoil from breaking the binding circle with a gun instead of just nudging the skull aside, struck Ferris down.

The circle, though, broke.

I surged forth, enveloping Cal in a wave of shadows, my claw-tipped fingers wrapping around his throat. He coughed out some words in a language I didn't recognise. The skin on my hands peeled away, flensed by magic. My blood dripped onto his perfectly-tailored suit, a darker colour than usual, with flecks of light shining throughout. Death's heart, combined with Reaper magic lending power to my blood.

I ignored the pain and squeezed harder, cutting off Cal's voice. He choked, scrabbling at me. I inhaled, closing my eyes. There was a scent, a tiny sense of something that didn't belong to the man in my grasp. My humanity.

"Give it back," I purred.

He scratched at my already-ruined hands, mouth searching for air like a fish gasping on the shore. His too-perfect looks, his tailored suit, his designer glasses, all of it was dishevelled. A mask. And beneath that mask? A frightened, desperate man. One who had been thrust into the world of magic and monsters without permission, without a choice in the matter. Who had tried to fix things so many times. Who had tried to make the world see him again, instead of quietly forgetting him. Who had, at first, wanted only to return to the way things were. Who had turned to mark, dark and terrible and forbidden, as a last resort.

I hissed through my teeth and let him go.

Cal sucked in a breath, then started coughing. He doubled over, spitting out blood, likely a result of his fight with Baz more than my own grasp. The sorcerer glared at me, and with a single tear that fell from his eyes, he became nothing more than a man. Human. As I once was.

My shadows folded in on themselves. My claws vanished. My skin became the pasty shade it usually was. My vision, though, remained grey and black and white. He still had my humanity.

"Go ahead," he spat. His hand trembled where it rested on the floor. "Kill me."

"I certainly could." It wouldn't be the first time I'd killed, no matter that I never took pleasure in such things. I still remembered the shock on the faces of the forgotten gods who had stood against me and lost. Cal, on the other hand, would be easy compared to their might. "You have done enough, caused enough, to warrant it. But as I have said before, I am a Reaper. The Man at the Crossroads. So I will give you one last choice. Return what you took, forswear your magic, and I will see to it that you are once again part of the fate of this world. You will be able to do all that you used to do. Work, talk with people, have a life. But you will never again be a part of Elsewhere or involve yourself with its people."

"Or?" Cal asked, the word spoken with venom.

"Or I will take what you stole by force. You will be an empty shell afterwards, if you survive. And I will take that empty shell to the darkest depths of Elsewhere, cursed to exist with an immortal's life, bound forever alone. In pain."

"This is the choice you offer me?" He sneered at me, that mask of arrogance and intent piecing itself back together even as I watched. I had a feeling I knew what he would choose, and I mourned for it. "Cruelty, to make me forswear all that I have accomplished in these last few years. And crueller, to make me exist in the emptiness. Some choice."

I gestured to the body of the siren. "What choice did you offer her? For that *cruelty* alone, I could easily offer you no choice at all. However, I recognise that this path was started by an act which you did not choose. A mistake. And while there are many injustices in the world, forcing things upon us that we would never choose, I will give you this choice. So, what will it be, Calvin Mason Thorp?"

Earlier that day, a young musician had chosen life, had chosen to fight for one more minute of music and inspiration. He had defied his heritage, his family, even the magic compelling him to act. And for that choice, he would struggle every day to play his music for an indifferent world. But he would pursue his dream.

This man before me, a mirror to myself had I been someone else, even for an instant, knelt on his knees, one hand braced on the floor while the other rubbed his injured throat, and he glared at me with every ounce of feeling he possessed. He wasn't fighting for a dream, for the hope of returning to the life he once had. He was fighting for revenge.

"What will it be?" I asked. The aura around him that told me of his lifeforce turned orange, then became sickly and weak.

"Screw you," he snarled.

A shame.

I reached out, my Reaper magic gathering at the tips of my fingers, and was about to touch him on his head, sealing the choice, when someone interrupted me.

"Cal, no!"

I turned, looking over my shoulder, only to see Neja standing there, one hand bound in rope, the other rubbed raw. Fury, plain and simple, rose in me. I spun back around to face the man and pressed my hand to his head.

The choice was made.

Reaper magic was unique in that I didn't always control the outcome. I offered a person a choice, they made it, and the magic took hold. In this instance, Cal had made his choice, so the magic took over, spreading to him through my touch like a virus, infecting every cell in his body, ripping the pieces he stole from me away from him. Only, I hadn't considered something.

Earlier, when Ferris shot him, *I* had been the one who died. We were linked, he and I, and in using my Reaper magic against him to separate my humanity from him, I also separated what remained from myself. The magic flowing through my veins tore myself apart. Violently.

Before, the blood magic spell had only stopped my human heart, scrubbing those few bits of humanity—the life that he wanted—from my veins. Now, my own magic reached inside the both of us and ripped my heart, *our* hearts, from my chest, pulling every last ounce of mortality from me along with it.

Cal screamed. I couldn't even find the breath to scream, my lungs crushed under the weight of pain. The both of us threw our heads back, bodies convulsing as something essential was torn away. I couldn't even name what it was that was taken, because as soon as it was gone, I had no words for it.

I died, terribly and with pain lighting up every nerve ending I had. But I could not die, not truly, and certainly not with Death's heart beating strongly in my chest. The only heart I possessed, now. White flashed before my eyes, and then I was awake, kneeling on the floor, hands covered in gore, healed of all hurt and harm.

Calm.

Steady.

There was a desperate longing in me for a thing I couldn't quite remember, but otherwise, I was me.

More or less.

Before me, the Other Cal lay on the floor, choking on blood that bubbled between his lips. His glasses were askew, and even without my Reaper sight veiling my eyes, I knew that he was dying. Despite the choice that he made, there would be no prison in the depths of Elsewhere. No, he would die on that floor, watching the person who stole his life walk away without a scratch.

Life wasn't fair.

"Are you alright?" Neja knelt beside me. She wasn't wearing a rope around her wrist anymore, but I could still see the redness where she'd been bound. She looked dishevelled, but other than the rope burns, I saw no injuries.

"I'm fine," I said. I blinked. My voice didn't sound quite the same. There was a different quality, a… serenity to it. One seated in the knowledge that eternity stretched before me, and that I had the power to claim it. "I feel a little different, perhaps."

Neja's eyes welled with tears. She brought up a hand to cup my cheek. "Oh, Cal. I tried to warn you. Blood magic binds victim and sorcerer together. You couldn't undo the spell unless he willingly gave back what he took, or if he died."

"If he was bound to me, then he couldn't die, because I cannot die." I looked at the man before me, shivering with blood loss, unable to form the words that might bring him a modicum of peace. I turned back to Neja. "Are we still linked?"

"No," she said, licking tears from where they fell across her lips. "No, you broke the binding by removing…by removing…what he stole from the both of you."

"My humanity." Ah. It hadn't been a dream, then. "My mortality. The last pieces of me that were something else."

Neja nodded. She rested her hand against my chest, where my singular heart, born of Death and now entirely my own, beat. I had the power of eternity in my blood. I was more than just a Reaper, now. But what, I didn't know.

"Oh, Cal, I'm so sorry," Neja breathed. I reached up and brushed a tear away.

"About what? I'm still here. I'm fine."

"You won't be you, not as you were. Not anymore."

"Then I'll be someone else." It didn't seem complicated to me, but perhaps that was something I'd lost. Gently, I moved Neja away from me and turned to the dying man. His mouth opened and closed, a whistle of air escaping. He was trying to say something, and failing. Why did he persist? Couldn't he understand that it was futile? Or was that a human trait, fighting against all odds?

Had I done that?

Surely not.

"For what it's worth," I said, inching closer, "I am sorry that things had to end this way. It is this senseless loss of life that had blood magic banned to begin with. You could have had everything you wanted, and yet you were determined to take revenge against me. Well, now you see the consequences of your actions."

Hurt and something like anger flashed in his eyes. He moved, his fingers reaching towards me, losing purchase in the blood that slicked across the floor. I took his hand. I wasn't sure if I wanted to apologise or ease his passing; after all, he really had been thrown into a situation that wasn't his choosing.

In the end, it didn't matter. The moment I touched his hand, he dissolved into dust. The last pieces of his humanity, burned away by my Reaper magic. It fell through my fingers like sand through a sieve, and I felt a brief moment of regret.

Then, I brushed my hands off, stood, and prepared to leave.

Only to find Baz bent over Special Agent Ferris. Her eyes were closed and her chest was barely moving, but she was alive. Her head was cradled in Baz's lap. He brushed his hands through her hair, and I thought he might be weeping. He looked up at me, fury burning through the sunglasses.

"This is your fault," he hissed.

"She chose to get involved," I pointed out. "And she will live—"

"Her back is broken! She landed across the table and broke her spine. I can *feel* it, the injustice of what was done to her because of this. Oh, yes, she *chose* to help you. To shoot that damn skull and set you free, and she did not deserve this as a reward."

"She lives," I repeated. Not harshly, just not understanding. Wasn't any life better than none?

"She is a Special Agent with the FBI. Her whole life has been devoted to the protection of law and justice. And now, for helping you, for helping me, she is broken. She will never fulfil her purpose again. Don't you feel even the tiniest shred of guilt for that?" Baz snarled. He clenched his fist into her hair, and she winced, but did not wake. He relaxed his hands, smoothing out the kinks he'd caused.

"Guilt will do nothing to change what happened," I said evenly. "I cannot change the past. Nor can I change the result of a choice, for good or ill."

Baz recoiled as if I'd personally struck him. "What happened to you?" he asked, emotion clogging his throat. "All I saw was shadow and fire and now you're... Cal, what did you do?"

"He ripped out the last pieces of his mortality," Neja said. "He was still bound to the other Cal when he tried to take his humanity back, and it, well, was removed from him as well. He's still Cal, but there's nothing human left. Not anymore."

Baz gaped at me. "Stars and stones," he breathed. "Cal, I'm sorry. I—"

"Don't be sorry," I said. "I'm fine. I may not be what I was, but I'm still me. Still here. And I still have a very great deal to do."

Baz didn't say anything, and by the set of his jaw I could tell that something I'd said unsettled him. I approached, and he tensed.

"I can't fix her." I nodded towards the fallen FBI agent. "I know she was one of yours, and that it means something to you, but I cannot change the outcome of her choices. I can, however, see that she has many more choices in her future."

A Reaper's gift. It was all I could give. So I did. A single mote of darkness, backed by the lights of possibility, floated through the air. It settled on Ferris' forehead, burning into her skin. She thrashed, as much as she could with a broken spine, and her face contorted with pain. But when she settled, when I looked at her again with my Reaper sight, I saw a myriad of choices spreading before her. Surgery to fix her spine, or life in a wheelchair. A life of love and family, or one of career and passion. Not all of the choices would be easy—choices rarely were—but they would be there.

"What do we do now?" Baz asked. He wasn't asking me, I realised, but Neja, who hovered by my side with nervous energy.

"Go back to Elsewhere," she suggested. "I think…I think this might need both Life and Death. They may have some answers. Something that can be done."

"Okay. Yeah. That's…that's good." Baz stood, giving Ferris one last sad look. "Do you think we could say goodbye to the band, first? They're at the hospital a few blocks from here. It just seems…I just want to say goodbye."

"I have no complaints to that plan," I said. "Neja?"

She shook her head. "That's fine."

Baz called the police, left a perfunctory message, then we left the coffee shop to the sound of sirens and shouts. Ferris would, hopefully, get the care she needed. The dead siren would likely remain unidentified, soon forgotten. Calvin Mason Thorp, on the other hand, would never have been there at all. I turned my back on the coffee shop and went to the hospital.

The band was just about ready to be released when we came upon them in Alice's room. There was a nurse doing one last test on Alice, but everyone else had been declared perfectly healthy. Valerie was noticeably absent, and when Jacques looked at me, there was devastation plain in his eyes. He'd learned of the cancer, then, as well as what had happened to her.

"Everyone alright?" Baz asked, giving Steve a fist bump and nodding to Richard and Bertie. Alice smiled eagerly, just a bit too happy.

"Yeah, we're great. We heard that the music festival

got shut down. The organisers are suing the various vendors, who are suing them in return. Word is that there's no real case, just a bunch of incompetent people coming together to do something they should have left well enough alone." Alice tossed her head, chuckling. "I guess we know who to call if we ever need to crash a party."

I waited for her to tell me who that would be and found all of them staring at me. I said nothing, and eventually they all looked away.

"Everything alright?" Jacques asked in an undertone to Baz and Neja. "He seems…scarier than usual."

"We'll fix it," Neja declared. Baz flinched.

"Is that even possible?" he whispered.

Neja shrugged and scuffed at the floor with her shoe. "I don't know, but we have to try."

"Whatever it is that is wrong, I hope you sort it out." Jacques held out a hand and Baz shook it. I did as well.

"Nothing is wrong," I corrected. "All the same, I thank you for your concern. And I wish you condolences about your grandmother. She was a kind woman."

Jacques scowled. "The best."

"It wasn't Grant's fault," Steve murmured. "Valerie—"

"Volunteered, I know. That doesn't mean I want to spend the next however long playing in a band with the kid."

"You offered Grant a gig?" Baz asked, brows rising well above the rims of his sunglasses.

"He's a good player," Alice said. "And he needed a

break. We'll see how it goes. Second guitar. Maybe he'll stay with us for a while, maybe he won't. Either way, we had to do something. After, you know, what Steve said his father did."

"That is merely the nature of the Fae," I pointed out. "Unfortunate, yes, but not surprising."

Again, they all looked at me. Neja threaded her arm through mine and offered a weak smile.

"We really do wish you the best," Baz said. The band all bobbed their heads and murmured thanks and words of friendship to my cousin, shaking hands and promising to keep in touch. They offered none of that to me.

Shortly after, Alice was officially discharged from the hospital, and it was decided we had better be on our way. Neja, Baz, and I found our way to an entrance to the Goblin Market and then to Elsewhere. It was better we didn't venture through Faerie to get home, after all.

I almost looked back as we left the mortal realm behind, that quiet longing pulling at me. I shook off the sensation and kept moving. It was done, and there was little point in looking back, hoping for something that I couldn't even name.

Little point at all.

It turned out that there was little point in summoning Life or Death to meet with us either, as they were waiting in front of my building on Death's lands when Neja, Baz, and I returned from the mortal realms. Yolanda and Agravane were plastered to the window in my advertising agency office, and I saw the flicker of blue that meant my pet miniature griffin ghost, Tempest, was watching for me in the flat above. I smiled fondly at that thought.

Life was unusually still, her hands resting calmly at her sides, her everchanging appearance subdued. Her presence sent reverberations through Death's lands, but even those felt less volatile than usual. Death, on the other hand, looked positively agitated. He was shifting his weight from foot to food, his hands first going to his pockets, then tugging at his cravat, then adjusting his pocket square or tugging at his sleeves. When he saw us approaching, he froze, empty eyes fixing on me with more emotion than I'd ever seen.

"So," Life said, looking me over. Her expression turned to stone. "It's done."

"You know what happened to him?" Neja asked, rushing forwards almost desperately. Baz put his hand on her shoulder to keep her back, but she shrugged him off.

"We know," Life said. To my surprise, she reached out and took Death's hand, twining their fingers together.

That answer, unsurprisingly, wasn't good enough for Neja. She rested a hand on her waist, fingers fiddling with the hilt of a throwing knife. She narrowed her eyes. "Explain. Because from where I'm standing, if you know what happened to him, then you could have done something about it. Made plans. Sent him with some sort of protection. You could have—"

"No." Life lifted her chin. "We could not have. If something else had happened to him, perhaps, but not this."

"Why not this?" Neja barked. "Why can't you fix *this*?"

Life looked me directly in the eye. "I'm sorry, Cal, that this happened to you."

"Don't be," I said, shrugging my shoulders. That quiet longing lingered at the back of my mind, but I was at peace. Life's sadness, Death's agitation, it meant very little to me except that it was unnecessary to be so distraught on my behalf.

"Please." Baz took a step towards the two most powerful entities in the realms. "He was my cousin. My family."

"And so he still is," Life said. She gestured to me. "He still stands there, still himself. He still retains his soul. There is not so much, ah, humanity about him, but in essence, in personality, he remains himself."

"Did you know this was going to happen?" Neja hissed, not bothering to turn her head and look at me. Was I that different? I felt like myself. I still had that inexorable longing, yes, but I still loved Neja and Baz, and I still wanted coffee to a perhaps unhealthy amount. I still wanted to do marketing. I still thought of Yolanda and Agravane as my closest friends. I was still me.

Wasn't I?

"We didn't know when, or who, but we knew that it would happen eventually." Life smiled at me, but the gesture was empty, flat. Even sad.

"I don't understand," I said.

Death lifted his head and looked at me. Into me. Through me. I saw the depths of his empty gaze and even a hint of what lay beyond. And for the first time since I'd been hired on by him, I wasn't afraid of that stare. He nodded. "It is difficult not to notice when a fundamental force of the universe comes into being."

Had I truly grasped what he was saying, perhaps I would have staggered back or swayed where I stood or something. Instead, I just stood there. Not understanding. Not comprehending.

"What do you mean?" Baz asked, breaking the silent tension that lay between us. "What's wrong with Cal?"

"Wrong?" Life scoffed. "Nothing is *wrong* with him. He is simply preparing to take my husband's place."

The heart I bore, the one that used to belong to Death, it beat in my chest with a solemn rhythm. One that nearly overwhelmed me with shadows and endings and pure, unadulterated power. My employer, the being who held the end of every living being in the palm of his hand, looked at me as if he could see that power beating in my chest.

"Everything dies, Cal," he murmured. "I've told you that from the beginning."

"But you…you're…you're Death!" Neja protested. She moved into me, as if by standing in front of me she could shield me from whatever path lay before me. "Surely you can't die."

"Not without someone equal, who has been prepared, to take my place. Not something that comes along every day, as you can probably imagine. I should have known," Death said, shaking his head. "I should have known that it would be you. That the last Reaper wouldn't just appear to me without cause. I thought you was just the interference of my mother, but you were—are—more. Human, but more. A Reaper who stands between myself and Life. Until you went on a journey to recover your lost soul and not only bound Fate, but placed my own heart in your chest. And now, with your humanity burned away, there is only that heart. Your Reaper nature was always precarious; so many of them became swayed towards Life or myself and thus became something else. You swayed towards me, in a way that I could never have predicted."

"But you're not dead. Not yet," I pointed out. Inside,

I was reeling. How could this have happened? How could *I* take Death's place?

"No, but I soon will be. And with me will go Life as you know her now, her mantle passed on to another." Death smiled, the look wan. "It is an inevitable cycle, Cal. Not one to protest or fight, but to acknowledge. Embrace."

"We can fix this," Neja said firmly. "We found Cal's *soul*. We can find a way to replace his humanity."

"No. You cannot." Life eyed Neja, her mouth twisted with contemplation. "There are some things that, once done, cannot be undone, my dear djinn."

"But—" Baz was immediately cut off.

"Enough." Death raised a hand, and all questions and arguments fell away. "This is not an event to happen tomorrow, or perhaps even in the next decade. It will be subtle, a slow transition. I will teach Cal all there is to know, and my wife will search for her own replacement. Then, in a year, or ten years, or a hundred years, she and I will simply cease to exist."

I was relieved. This wasn't happening right away. I had time.

Did I even want this? It certainly didn't appear that my opinion was involved in the situation at hand. Sorting out something like that would likely take more than one evening spent curled over a cup of coffee. It was a solitary activity, not one to explore with several people staring at me, as they were then.

So I did the only thing I could. I asked, "What do I do?"

Death smiled, the expression genuine. "For now,

you transition your marketing work over to Agravane and Yolanda full time. We start training you as my apprentice. You will have to establish your own power base, acquire allies, determine your own methods of performing your duties, but for now, you'll just shadow me."

"Acquire allies…" I licked my lips, memories of me losing my temper over the last few days filling my mind. Certainly there were very few people I'd met during this last trip that would count themselves as my allies. "I encountered a Faerie who called himself the Shadow King."

Life's face twisted. "Him. Stars, what a bore. Tries to paint himself as a glorious fixer, but really he just tries to strike terror into those with less power than he so they'll do his bidding. Tacky."

Baz heaved a sigh, though it sounded like affectation more than genuine. "Cal, where are you going with this?"

"Before sending him back to Faerie, he revealed some, ah, interesting information. About the other Reapers. He suggested they had been trapped."

Life and Death both gaped at me. If my coming back as Death's successor had distressed them, this left them entirely gobsmacked.

"Where?" Death croaked.

"How?" Life demanded.

"He said they were bound somewhere beyond the land of the dragons by fallen gods. Said that I needed to talk with the Fisher King." I shrugged. "I had a few other things on my mind at the time, and I didn't ask for details."

Death was suddenly right before me, inches away, eyes blazing with power and barely restrained fury. "Your first task as my apprentice," he murmured in a deadly tone, "will be to find the other Reapers. To free them. And to bring whoever did this to me in chains. Are we understood?"

I nodded, a healthy dose of fear dancing up my spine. "We are understood."

Before I could ask more questions—such as who would even *want* to cross both Life and Death—they were gone. Neja leaned into me as if she'd been using all her strength to stand upright while confronting the two essential forces of the universe.

"What are you going to do?" she asked, voice shaking.

"Right now? I'm going to go upstairs, take the world's hottest shower, have a gallon of coffee, and then figure out how in the world I'm going to rescue a bunch of Reapers from a mysterious enemy, when I don't even know where they are or how to find them. You?"

Neja snorted. She wiped a hand against her eye, leaving smudges of tears behind. "Glad you're still in there, Cal."

"I never left, Neja," I said, kissing the crown of her head. "I swear."

She stiffened for a moment, then relaxed against me. "Didn't you?"

I didn't have an answer for her, only that same

longing that settled in my chest, filling an empty spot where my human heart used to be. It was quieter, now, but deeper in ways that I wasn't ready to explore. So instead, I pulled away from Neja, nodded to Baz, and headed towards my building.

"Come on," I said. "We have to go explain things to Yolanda and Agravane. We'd better order food, too. It's going to be a long night."

ACKNOWLEDGMENTS

I could never have written this book without my strangely expansive childhood musical education. To the person who is responsible for my random spouting of musical quotes when in opportune circumstances, I say thank you.

Also, a huge thanks to my cover designer, Fay, who has done all the books for this series and is completely amazing! She has taken my slightly ridiculous vision and turned it into a reality.

For those readers who are always happy to read this sort of thing and call it entertaining, I thank you. I am fully aware that it's nonsense, but it's fun nonsense, so here we all are. To be fair, you all seem to like this nonsense.

There are, in truth, so many people who come together for the writing of a book. I cannot possibly thank you all, so I will express my general gratitude and hope that one day, I can buy you a cup of hot chocolate.

ABOUT THE AUTHOR

Evelyn Grimald "E.G." Stone is an independent author, editor, and linguist who has been writing, creating and causing vast amounts of trouble since a young age. When not writing, she is off musing about the workings of languages - both real and created - or drawing and sewing. E.G. reads voraciously, perhaps to the point of slight-insanity. Weird, nerdy, perhaps a little crazy, she is having a grand old time writing, reading, editing, musing on language, and, naturally, continuing her endeavours in causing trouble.

ALSO BY E.G. STONE

<u>The Wing Cycle:</u>
The One Who Could Not Fly
To Never Hear the Song
The Forsaking of the Blind

<u>On Behalf of Death:</u>
The Innocence of Death
Knowledge Aforethought
A Party of Certainties
When Death's Away
Mischief, Mayhem, and Shakespeare
The Long Way Home
Miss You When You're Gone
Me, Myself, and I

The Order of the Owl
The Crow and the King
Speaker of Words